MR. MAY

Calendar Boys Series

NICOLE S. GOODIN

Mr. May
Published by Nicole S. Goodin
ISBN: 978-0-9951168-9-4
Copyright 2019 by Nicole S. Goodin
All rights reserved. ©
First published May 2019

Cover design by Nicole Goodin
Images purchased from Deposit Photos
Editing by Spell Bound

For all the babes born in May

CHAPTER ONE

Jake

The commentator's booming voice stretches along the sand and out into the water before us.

"Up in this final, we have one of our most competitive rivalries. Surfing in the blue jersey, we have Zeke Brady, currently ranked number two on this leg of the tour. And coming up against him, in the yellow leader's jersey, we have Jake Carson. You're going to want to sit up and pay attention here, folks, these two guys have a tendency to fight to the bitter end."

He goes on to rattle off some stats and whatever other drivel he deems important.

It doesn't matter what else some guy has to say.

It's just me, Zeke and the waves.

I rub a little more wax into my board and then toss it on top of my towel.

I tug my board under my arm and approach the water's edge.

I can see Zeke out of the corner of my eye, on my right.

"You ready, Brady?" I smirk at him.

He dutifully ignores me, but I don't miss the tick of his jaw.

I chuckle and shake my head.

"Always so tense, maybe that's your problem, bro, you need to relax. Maybe then you'll finally get a win."

"We're just waiting on the jet skis so we can get these surfers in the water and get this final under way," the commentator informs the crowd.

I can hear people calling my name as I stretch out my muscles, preparing to throw myself into the ocean.

"Keep an eye out here for Jake to take the lead early, that's his style and he'll be going for priority out there ahead of Zeke."

We're close now.

I can almost feel the ocean engulfing me already.

I turn, my eyes scanning the crowded beach for one person in particular.

The beach is packed today – everyone in town has come out to get a slice of the action.

I find her standing at the front of the crowd, looking directly at me.

She knows this part of the routine as well as I do.

I stare directly at her and bring my hand up to my mouth.

I blow her a kiss and shoot her the grin I know drives her wild.

I watch her gasp – she can't seem to help it – even though this is miles from the first time we've done this.

She composes herself and slowly lifts her hand towards her face.

Here it is.

I might even enjoy this part more than the waves I can hear crashing behind me.

She lifts her middle finger in the air and points it in my direction, her expression shooting daggers.

I chuckle as I turn back around, just in time for the skis to appear in front of us, waiting to take us out into the line up.

"*Damn*... your sister looks bangin' today, bro," I taunt Zeke as I run out into the crashing waves.

"I'll kill you," I hear him yell after me.

I laugh louder. I'd like to see him try.

CHAPTER TWO

Eden

"Fuck him, you'll get him next time, Z."

"Language," he snaps at me.

I roll my eyes. "I'm not a child anymore. You can relax, it's hardly the first time I've cursed."

In fact, I curse like a trucker – I really don't know why he even bothers.

He leans his board up against the fence and steps under the shower, effectively halting our conversation.

I hate it when he loses. Not that coming second is technically losing, but nonetheless, he didn't win.

Jake did. *Again.*

The guy is on fire at the moment, and Zeke hates bringing up the rear, especially when it's to Jake.

"Where's Millie?" I ask loudly, so he can hear me over the spray of the shower.

"She's still down on the beach I think," he yells back.

Thank god for that. She's the only one that he'll listen to when he's in a mood, and I'm more than happy to let her take over from here.

"You gonna head down to see her?" I ask him.

Hint, hint.

"Yeah, I gotta check in with coach and then I'll go track her down."

I nod my head at him. "Well then... if you're all good, I'm going to find River."

"I'm fine, Eden. You can go hang out with your friends."

He puts his head under the stream of water and lets it run down his face.

A group of girls walk past, and I don't miss the way they eye-fuck my older brother. They whisper to one another and giggle like little school girls.

I roll my eyes again.

"Friggin' groupies," I mutter under my breath.

I'm *so* glad Zeke finally settled down with Millie. For a while there he was making a good show of sleeping his way through half the beach like a total man whore.

Not that I blame him. It would be one hell of a distraction with all these half-naked, tanned bodies strolling around. Not that I'd ever get that opportunity to explore any of them.

Not with the overprotective big brother lurking around.

He chuckles and shakes his head at me. Maybe the insult wasn't under my breath after all.

"Go," he insists as he shuts off the water. "Seriously. I'm fine."

I nod. "You did really well today, you should be proud. I know I am."

He smiles at me, and it melts my heart. He should try smiling more often. Grumpy old bastard is always wearing a scowl.

"Thanks, sis. Now get out of here."

He lunges for me, no doubt to pull me into a wet hug, but I dart out of the way and up the steps, looking for River.

"Don't forget about the bonfire tonight," he calls after me.

I wave out in acknowledgement.

As if I would have forgotten. There's no way me and River will be missing that.

When they all cut loose and chill out is the only time they loosen the reins and we get to have any real fun.

River's brother, Alexi Moraz, is on the tour with Zeke.

I search the deck for her pitch-black hair. She's bound to be around here somewhere.

Alexi got knocked out in the semi-finals, and he rarely lets her hang out on the beach without him.

I think Zeke is bad, but he's got *nothing* on Alexi.

"Eden!" I hear her voice call out. I turn slowly until I spot her, sitting with Sierra and Jay.

Their brothers are on the tour too, but unlike River and me, they don't go everywhere with the crew. They mostly come out on weekends and holidays – days like today.

I wave to them excitedly and rush over to the spot they've claimed on the crowded deck.

Some of the guys are still out in the water, surfing for fun – because apparently being out there all day competing isn't quite enough.

I swear most of them have sea water running through their veins.

"Hey!" I say as I reach the girls and slide my ass into the only free chair.

"How's Zeke?" Sierra asks quickly, and I have to refrain from rolling my eyes for a third time in the space of ten minutes.

"*Grumpy.*" I sigh. "He'll be fine. He's going to see Millie – she'll improve his mood."

Sierra tries to cover her disappointment with a smile that fools absolutely no one.

It's no secret that she has a giant crush on my brother. She always has. Even though he's never looked at her as anything other than his little sister's friend or his mate's baby sister.

Sierra, just like me and the other two girls sitting here, are firmly off limits for any guy on the tour.

They all have some bullshit unwritten rule.

Sure, the ones without sisters are more inclined to break those rules, but that didn't stop Jay's older brother Max from kicking a guy's ass last season anyway.

For a bunch of laid-back surfer dudes, they have absolutely no chill when it comes to their sisters.

If you'd listen to my brother, I'm off limits for *any* guy, *ever*, not just the ones on this tour, but what he doesn't know won't hurt him. I'm not going to be eighty, all alone with my fifteen cats, just to please him.

No fucking way.

"Jake is on some serious form this year." River shakes her head as she watches a replay of the final on the screen on the side of the deck area. "It's like he can't put a foot wrong out there."

She's not wrong, as much as I can't stand the guy, I have to admit, he's killing it right now.

Zeke is in the best shape of his life right now, surfing better than he ever has, and he's still struggling to keep up with Jake. I can understand why he's getting so pissed off.

Fucking Jake.

Every god damn time he comes up against my brother he *has* to do it.

He taunts him by blowing me a freaking kiss.

I've tried to ignore it, I really have, but I can't seem to ignore *him*.

My eyes always find his, I think some sick, twisted little part inside me almost likes it.

It doesn't hurt that he's gorgeous – even if he knows it – the assholes always seem to be the best-looking ones.

"Hey, Eden."

I turn and find Lukah, walking by our table.

"Hey, nice ride out there today," I tell him, even though I didn't see his apparent near-perfect ride for myself.

"Yeah, it was awesome, Lukah," River chimes in.

His cheeks colour and he bumps his knee into a chair. He's not looking where he's walking, instead he's still looking at River.

The girls erupt into fits of laughter, and I try my hardest not to join in and embarrass him further.

"I'll see you around," I call out to him. He looks like he wants the ground to reach up and swallow him whole.

He's a rookie on the tour this year, and he's young. His crush on her is becoming as obvious as Sierra's is on my brother.

"Awww, he's so cute," River coos.

"He's all yours." I giggle. "Put the poor boy out of his misery already."

Her cheeks pink and it makes me wonder if maybe she's not totally against the idea of a bit of that action.

I'm about to put her on the spot when I hear *his* voice. We had to speak of the god damn devil, didn't we?

"Well, if it isn't the 'baby sisters' club'... what's happening ladies?"

I debate saying nothing, but I just don't have it in me to ignore him.

The asshole has called us the 'baby sisters' club' for years, even though there's nothing much baby about any of us anymore.

I twist around so I can see him – and that's my first mistake.

His hair is half wet, half dry and dishevelled in that sexy way of his.

He's shirtless, his firm, toned torso on full display, and my eyes devour it like the greedy little bastards they are.

He's in his classic attire. A pair of board shorts, and absolutely *nothing* else.

I really don't want to like what I see, but unfortunately, my hormones didn't get that particular memo.

At least I had the good sense to wear sunglasses, so my eye-fuck is my little secret.

My next mistake is engaging with the enemy.

I know it's a bad idea, but once again, I can't seem to help myself.

He infuriates me to the point where I can't see reason. Half the time he wears an expression that lets you know he doesn't give a shit who you are or what you think of him, and there's some small part, deep inside me, that insists upon trying to wipe that look off his face.

"*Jake*," I reply sweetly. "You should ask your sponsor for some new shirts."

He chuckles. "I thought about it, but I didn't want to deprive you of the sight."

"You know what? I think I'd survive," I drawl.

"You owe me a kiss." He smirks, jumping right into his torture, his face a smug mask.

I cross my arms across my chest, and I don't miss the way his eyes dip down to my cleavage before moving back to my face.

I might want to punch him, but at least I get the satisfaction of knowing that he's noticed I'm all grown up now.

"When hell freezes over," I retort.

He wraps his arms around his body, running his hands up and down his sides. "Brrrr."

"Clever."

"No worries, precious, I'll just put it on your tab with all the others."

The use of the stupid nickname he's dubbed me with only adds fuel to my fire.

"I'll tell you what you can do, you can shove it up your—"

"Annnnd I think it's time to go," River interrupts me, dragging me away by my arm.

"You're such an asshole," I hiss at him.

"Assholes need love too." He smirks.

I don't know why I have to do this – let him antagonise me this way.

I should have learnt my lesson last season.

I glare over my shoulder at him as the girls flank me, leading me away from him.

"Cocky wanker," I call out while he can still hear me.

"Brat," he calls back, playing into our little game of to and fro.

I can hear his egotistical laugh and it makes my blood boil.

He smirks and waves at me as we disappear down the stairs.

"Stupid, arrogant bastard," I grumble.

"Girrrrrrl... you're going to get yourself into trouble with that boy." River giggles as we lose sight of him.

"What is that meant to mean?" I snap at her.

"It means, he doesn't just want to ride the waves, if you know what I'm sayin." She waggles her brows suggestively, and I flip her off.

The girls all giggle as though they've heard some joke I'm not privy to.

CHAPTER THREE

Jake

"I'll give you credit, man, even I can't tell if you love her or hate her."

I raise my brow at Max and take a pull of my beer.

I don't want to give him an answer one way or the other.

Giving any answer would reveal that I give a shit when the last thing I want to do, is give a shit.

Right now, I'm just happy to have him think I enjoy winding her brother up – and truthfully, I do, as childish as that might be.

I glance back at her; she's sitting over the other side of the fire with her little girly gang, wearing nothing more than a bikini and some see-through scrap of a dress.

I'll have to find out who makes that thing, so I can write them a letter of appreciation, because *fuck* she looks good wearing it.

"*Dude.*" Max nudges my knee. "Don't do it, man, he'll kill you. You know he will."

I chuckle. "He's told me as much." My eyes flicker from Eden to her brother Zeke.

He's not paying attention. He's had a few drinks now – drowning his sorrows it looks like.

Any one of these guys is competition on their best days, but Zeke – he's competition *every* day. Maybe that's why I have so much fun pissing him off.

13

He makes it too easy to get inside his head – and Eden, she's his biggest weakness.

One I'm totally willing to exploit. Whether it's for his benefit or my own.

"Your funeral," he mutters as he gets to his feet.

I know he's not messing around. A bunch of the boys had to deal to Fitzy last year because he got a little bit too up close and personal with Max's sister, Jay.

Personally, I didn't think it was a problem that he fucked her – she's a grown woman – but there was no telling Max that.

The 'baby sisters' club' are untouchable out here. Or at least that's what the boys like to think.

I smirk to myself at their stupid law.

I've always enjoyed breaking the rules.

She glances around then, almost as though she can feel my eyes on her.

She eventually finds me, and I don't even try to hide my stare. I don't care. It gives me a thrill when she catches me undressing the little she's got on with my eyes.

She glares at me and turns her head away, her long blonde hair swishing around her shoulders like a little princess.

I chuckle and get to my feet. "Max, wait up!" I call after him as I jog across the sand. "I'll keep it in my pants tonight, I promise."

"Just tonight?" he calls back to me.

"Hey, I'm no saint." I chuckle.

"I'm going for a night surf," he announces when I reach him. "You in?"

"Hell yeah, I'm in."

He holds his fist out to me and I bump my knuckles against his.

***

I've always found peace out in the water.

No one seems to be able to figure out how I stay so relaxed, so cool under pressure, but it's because I simply don't feel the pressure.

I just surf.

Every ride is different than the next and it's a privilege to be out here on the water.

I'm not about to ruin it by overthinking it or stressing about scores while I'm out here.

I ride every wave like it's my last, and that seems to be where I find my edge.

I'm the best, I know I am, and if that earns me the cocky reputation that I've been dubbed with on the beach, then so be it – because they all know I'm the best too.

That yellow leader's jersey hasn't left my side since I first got handed it, and I don't plan on giving it up any time soon either.

Surfing is my whole life. I can't imagine going more than a day or two without hitting the water.

I'd lose my mind.

This is my home out here.

Even now, with only the light of the moon to see the incoming sets, and the fire of the beach to use as a landmark, I've never been more comfortable.

So many people fear the ocean, and I agree that a healthy amount of fear is a good thing, but it's respect that you really need to have.

The minute you don't respect the ocean, you're screwed.

"Jake! We're heading in!" one of the boys yells out across the breakers to me.

"One more ride," I holler back.

I look over my shoulder. There's a set coming in soon. Third wave from the back is the winner.

I paddle myself into position and wait for the rush of water.

I feel it. I don't even bother looking, and before I know it, I'm on my feet, surfing all the way back into the shore. Pulling tricks that come as naturally to me as walking.

I pick up my board off the sand and glance up at the fire.

The crowd has thinned out considerably.

I undo my leg rope and I'm just about to follow up the sand after the other guys when I hear yelling.

Screaming would be a better word for that noise, actually.

I look down the beach, and I think I can make out a group of people running towards the water.

"Drunk idiots," I hiss as I drop my board on the sand and jog down the beach towards the sound.

I don't know what they're up to, but if they've been drinking, they shouldn't be near the water.

We all know that.

They're about twenty metres away when I figure out what's happening. A group of guys has hold of a girl, and they're about to toss her in the sea by the looks of things.

Harmless enough I guess, but probably not the smartest move if she's anywhere near as drunk as they appear to be.

I get a little closer and I notice who it is they've got and that she's screaming and clawing at their arms.

It's Eden, and she's terrified.

"Take me back, *please*, just take me back," she screams.

I close the gap between myself and them within a second.

It's only once I'm right behind them that I see her friends are there too, jumping at the guys' arms, begging them to let her down.

It's Joe, Steve and Mark.

They're in waist-deep water, holding her above their heads like she's some kind of offering to the ocean.

She's begging them again, and I have no idea why she's freaking out so much, but she is. She's petrified.

"Jake, help!" Sierra begs, as she notices me behind her.

"Put her the fuck down," I say calmly.

The guys' laughter dies down as they all turn and look at me.

"We're just having a bit of fun with her, golden boy."

They've still got her above their heads, and when my eyes meet hers, I see nothing but fear shining in the moonlight.

"She's not having fun. Put her down."

Joe shrugs. "Down she goes, lads."

"No!" I hear the girls shriek at the same moment that the guys toss her in the sea.

"Go to bed, you little assholes," I growl at them as they wade back out of the water, high-fiving each other like the absolute idiots they are.

I turn back and see the 'baby sisters' club' is in a panic. They're madly splashing at the water, and Eden isn't with them.

"What the fuck are you doing?"

"We can't find her!" Sierra shrieks, and it's genuine panic.

I stride towards them, looking desperately for Eden, but they're right, she's not there.

"Stop splashing," I demand before I dive under the water.

I can't see fuck all, it's so dark out, and they've churned up all the sand with their frantic splashing.

I feel around for her but come up empty.

I don't know what the fuck is happening here. Did she hit her head? Can she not swim? None of this makes sense. She lives her life surrounded by the sea – of course she can swim.

I push back up to the surface and suck in another breath before going back under. I reach around in the darkness again, and this time I find her.

I drag her above the water with me, and my heart races as she chokes and splutters.

Thank god.

I scoop her up into my arms and carry her back to the shore as she coughs and gasps for air.

I can hear the girls splashing around, following after me.

"Is she okay?" River appears in front of me.

I stop on the wet sand and sit down with her in my lap. "She's breathing."

River starts crying – in relief I assume. Sierra and Jay make it up next to her and wrap their arms around River.

All three look shaken as hell.

"Which one of you is going to tell me what the fuck happened here? Why didn't she just stand up?"

She could have easily touched the bottom. I know she hasn't hit her head. She didn't go in head-first for starters and it's all sand underfoot out there anyway. There was nothing for her to have hit.

They all look at each other knowingly, but none of them seem willing to speak.

"Can't she swim?"

I'm about to bark another demand at them when River speaks up and shakes her head. "No... she can't swim."

I have a pretty good idea that she's bullshitting me, but Eden chooses that moment to open her eyes, so I don't push it. Not right now anyway.

"Hey, precious, are you okay?"

Her eyes widen and she gasps for breath.

"Relax," I instruct. "Just nice and easy. You swallowed some water."

She does what I tell her, her wide blue eyes never leaving mine as she breathes slowly in and out.

"Where the fuck is Zeke?" I ask the girls, without looking up.

"He got *wasted*. Millie took him to bed. Eden wanted to stay," one of them explains.

Sierra races up the beach and comes back with a bunch of bags in her hands.

I inhale deeply through my nose. *Fucking Zeke.* He should have had her back.

He's always keeping tabs on her when she doesn't need it, and now, when she could have actually benefitted from his protective bullshit, he's nowhere to be seen.

This might have been all fun and games to those pricks on the beach, but this clearly wasn't fun for her.

"Where's Alexi?" I ask the question directed at River. Her older brother would never leave her alone out here for long... pissed or not.

"He just went to put away his board. He was going to walk us home when he got back."

I nod. "Good. Have him take the three of you. I'll take care of Eden."

"I'm okay," Eden says as she tries and fails to sit up.

"You're drenched, and I'm pretty sure you've been drinking."

"I've been in the water?" she asks, her voice a whisper and that same fear in her eyes again.

I nod my head.

She faints.

"Eden!" Jay shrieks.

"She's fine," I say as I roll her on her side in my arms. "She's just fainted. She'll be okay."

"River?!" I hear someone calling from up the beach. "Where are you?"

"That's Alexi," River says anxiously. "He'll come looking if I don't go."

"Go," I tell the three of them. "Tell him Eden went home while he was gone, alright?"

Sierra places a bag on Eden's lap and looks at me with scared eyes.

They all get to their feet and scamper away without questioning my authority.

"Jake?" River stops and calls back to me. "Look after her, okay? Please?"

I nod at her. I might be an asshole to this woman most of the time, but I'm not too much of a prick that I wouldn't make sure she was safe after this ordeal – not that I understand what the hell is going on.

I wait for the girls to disappear up the beach before getting to my feet – Eden in my arms.

I carry her along the sand, somehow managing to collect my abandoned board as I go, all the way back to my room.

CHAPTER FOUR

Eden

I wake up with a start.

I dreamed I was under the water... and that I couldn't find my way back up. I could see the stars in the night sky above me, but no matter how much I wanted to push up, I couldn't do it, almost as if there was an invisible layer between me and my next breath.

I'm covered in a thin layer of sweat and my breathing is rapid.

I inhale deeply to try and ease my racing heart before opening my eyes.

It's brighter in here than it has been every other morning.

I roll over and the sight in front of me causes my already speeding pulse to sky rocket further.

It's the yellow leader's jersey, tossed over a chair in the corner of the room.

"No, no, no, no, no," I chant in a whisper.

I can't be here. In *his* room.

Where the fuck is Zeke?

This has to be a mistake, but when I find the courage to look around further, it only cements the fact that this is no mistake.

This is Jake Carson's room.

Jake Carson's bed. And I'm in it.

I look down, and holy shit, I'm wearing a man's t-shirt. There's no prizes for guessing who it belongs to.

What have I done?

I slip my hands under the t-shirt and praise the lord, I've still got my bikini on.

That's something at least.

I was wearing a dress last night. I may have had a couple of drinks, but I know that much for certain.

I glance around the room, looking for it, trying my hardest not to move a muscle.

I'm too scared to look to my left, just in case I'm not alone in this bed.

"Hey."

His voice startles me. It didn't come from the bed next to me though, so that's a relief. I scan the room until I see him, lying on the couch.

"Hey," I reply nervously.

It might only be one word each, but this is the most civilised conversation we've ever had.

"You're awake," he says, and I don't know what happened last night, but he's looking at me with a... *softness* in his expression. I don't know what the hell that's all about, and I instantly am wary of it.

"I am."

I don't know what series of events led me to wind up in my enemy's bed, but it would seem I'm going to have to shame myself by asking the question.

I didn't think I had more than a couple of beers last night, but everything seems... *hazy*.

"Did we... um... did we have sex?" I ask with a wince.

He chuckles and sits up. The blanket he had covering him pools around his waist, and *damn*, he's deliciously topless, yet again.

He shakes his head, and relief washes over me. "Trust me, you'd remember if we did," he replies, his tone cocky.

This is the Jake I'm used to. Not the one looking at me with concern.

"Why am I wearing your shirt?" I demand, finding a bit of my confidence now that I know I didn't sleep with him last night.

He runs his hand through his shaggy hair and yawns. "Your dress was wet."

He points, and I follow the gesture to an open window in the corner. I see my dress hanging on the window frame.

I scuttle out of bed and grab it. I should probably go into the bathroom to change, but realistically, I'm pretty confident he put me in this shirt – and half the world has seen me in a bikini by now anyway, so I decide to save myself some time and do it right here.

It's over my head before it registers exactly what he's said.

"How'd it get wet?" I ask cautiously as I slip my dress into place.

Memories start flooding in before he can even answer me.

It wasn't just a dream. I *was* in the water.

Holy shit.

"A couple of the guys tossed you in the sea."

My blood turns to ice.

"I had to fish you out... can't you swim?"

I feel like I'm going to hurl.

I was in the ocean.

I was under the water.

He had to pull me out.

It was just like my dream – I wasn't coming back up on my own.

I cover my mouth and run for the bathroom. I barely make it to the toilet before I throw up noisily.

"Eden? Are you okay?" I hear him ask from the doorway, his voice panicked.

"Just leave me, please, Jake. I'll be okay."

"Precious?"

"Please go," I beg.

I hear him shut the door behind me.

I wipe my mouth and swipe at the hot, angry tears that are rolling down my face.

I take five deep breaths, just like my therapist has told me to do, and with each exhale, I reassure myself that I'm okay, that I'm safe, that I'm alive.

It hits me then, what I have somehow managed to get myself into... Jake has just seen me at my absolute worst, and with a mouth the size of his, the whole tour is bound to hear all about it by lunch time.

I flush the toilet and squeeze a bit of his toothpaste onto my finger to try and get rid of my bad breath.

I look at my bloodshot eyes and messed-up hair in his mirror.

I look like shit.

I need to talk to River. I need to find out what the fuck happened last night from someone that isn't him, because right now, it appears I owe my life to this boy, and I'm not sure how I feel about that.

I open the bathroom door slowly, hoping like hell that maybe he's not going to be in here waiting, but of course he is.

He's sitting on the edge of his bed, his expression wary as he looks up at me.

I don't like wary on him. I don't know how to deal with it. I'd give anything for his usual arrogance right now.

"Are you okay?"

I give him what I hope is a convincing smile. "I'm fine. I must have had too much to drink last night. I'm sorry you had to see that."

I look around for any sign that I was wearing something on my feet, but find none, so I take a couple of steps in the direction of the door, eager to be as far away from here as humanly possible. I spot my bag on the way and snag it from the floor.

He looks less than convinced by my explanation.

"You're lying."

He's right. I am.

"Really, I'm good. Thank you for helping me out, but you can go back to making my life hell now. I'm fine," I ramble.

I step towards the door again and stumble on the leg rope of one of his boards.

"Eden." It's almost a plea.

I ignore him and make it the rest of the way to the door; I slip out without so much as a backwards glance.

***

I try to turn the key as quietly as possible to my room. I share a suite with Zeke and Millie, and the last thing I need is my big brother on my case about where I spent the night.

"Just leave it, she's a grown woman," I hear Millie hiss as I tip toe inside.

I drop my head in defeat.

They're awake and they're aware I've been missing.

"I can't," Zeke hisses back. "She's my little sister."

I hear Millie mutter something else, but I don't catch what it was.

"Eden, where the hell have you been?" he calls out.

"Stayed with River," I say, and I hope like hell it's the right answer.

Not because he's in charge of me and what I do, but because I don't want him to know what happened last night with the guys... or with Jake. *Definitely* not what happened with Jake.

He'd kill the lot of them.

I can remember what happened around the bonfire now. Bits and pieces came flooding back to me on my short walk home.

I was being a smart ass. We all were. We'd had a few drinks and were running our mouths.

If the guys had have picked up *any* of the other girls, it would have been nothing more than a funny joke.

But instead, they chose me.

They didn't know about me and my fear of the water, but I still can't stop myself from hating them a little bit for it.

I could have drowned.

If it weren't for Jake, I might have.

I feel a pang of guilt for the way I ran out on him just now. I'm not even sure if I said thank you to him for saving me.

I run my hands over my face.

"Any more questions?" I yell out down the hall to where I can hear Zeke and Millie arguing in whispers again.

"Not for now," he eventually answers.

"Maybe if you hadn't got yourself written off, you'd know the answers already," I push my luck by saying.

He's a hypocrite really. He can't judge me when he's out there drinking himself stupid and doing god knows what else.

I rush down the hall and into my room before he decides he does, in fact, want to ask me anything more. No sense in tempting fate.

The minute I'm in the safety of my room, I pull my phone out of my bag and hit dial on River's name.

I can see I've got a bunch of texts from her and a few from Jay and Sierra too, but I'll read them after.

"Eden?" she answers on only the third ring.

"Hey."

"Oh, *thank god*, I've been so worried about you."

"I'm okay. I just got back to my room."

"You stayed with Jake?"

I breathe a sigh of relief, at least one of us seems to know what happened last night, even if she does sound surprised I spent the whole night.

"I woke up in his room."

"He saved you, Eden. We were trying to find you, but you didn't come up. It was dark and the waves kept coming in..."

Her voice is trembling, and I feel terrible for having scared her like this.

"I'm sorry," I whisper.

"It's not your fault." She sobs.

"I'm fine, seriously. I'm okay."

"I was so scared. We *all* were."

"Thanks for having my back," I say through the lump in my throat. River is the best friend I've ever had, and I hate that I've put her though this.

She gains composure of herself again.

"I'll always have your back, but it's not me you should be thanking, it's Jake."

"I know."

"It was so strange. He comes across as so cocky, but you should have seen him. He came out of nowhere – he must have heard you screaming, and he demanded they put you down."

I don't remember anything much from the exact moment in time she's referring to. My brain has a solid habit of blocking out distressing experiences.

"So they did. That's when we panicked, we couldn't find you in the water and he was so calm. He just dived under and pulled you out. He was so gentle with you; he carried you in his arms and sat you in his lap."

I feel my cheeks blushing. I'm humiliated.

"He was really sweet, Eden. Maybe he's not as bad as you think he is."

I don't even know what to think anymore.

He's still the asshole that taunts my brother and winds me up to no end, but River's right, much like the roaring ocean, there's more under the surface when it comes to Jake Carson.

"I'll be sure to thank him today."

"I think I'll do the same," she replies.

"I told Zeke I stayed with you, okay, so go along with it if he mentions anything?"

"There might be one problem with that."

I groan. Of course there is. "What?"

"Alexi." I can almost hear her grimacing. "He walked me and the girls back. If Zeke talks to him, he's going to know you lied."

I rake my hand over my face.

"I guess I'll just hope he doesn't."

It frustrates me to no end that I can't just be honest with my brother about things like this, but the reality is, I can't.

Even though I understand his reasons for being protective, it's way past time for *him* to understand that I'm all grown up now. I'm not ten years old anymore, and I don't need him to keep me protected every five seconds – no matter how much last night might suggest otherwise.

"I'm sure it'll be fine," she reassures me.

I doubt that's true, but it is what it is.

I'll deal with the fall out if and when it happens.

"Can you meet me down the beach in an hour?" I ask her.

"I'll be there."

I finish up talking to River and then strip off yesterday's clothes.

I've got a photo shoot this afternoon, but this morning is all mine.

We'll be heading out on the road again tomorrow – moving to a new location for the next stop on the tour before a two-week break.

I throw on a new bikini and a light blue dress that I got given last week.

That's the biggest perk to being a model – the free shit.

The down side is that the surf brand I model for specialises in swim wear... and I clearly don't swim, but at least I look good standing on the beach.

I toss my phone on the bed and head out the door.

I wait until I get to the front door before I yell out to Zeke. "Heading down the beach, I'll be back later."

I don't wait for a reply before closing it behind me.

***

I stand at the water's edge, just my feet being lapped at by the warm ocean water.

This is furthest I'm willing to go.

I watch him ride the wave as though the board is an extension of him. He's so in tune with the waves, the sets, the movement of the ocean in general... I hate to admit it, but he really is the best. I doubt there's a better surfer in the world than him right now.

He's a freak.

He'll be the world champion this year. I can just feel it.

He drops super deep into the pipe, disappearing from my sight for a few beats before coming out clean, he winds up again from the bottom, hacking at the face of the wave, before shaking out his hair and grinning.

He hasn't even seen me, and there's no one else in the water yet, so I know his smile is genuinely because he loves what he does. It's not for the crowd, the cameras or his opponent. It's just for him.

He lives for the waves.

He looks like he chuckles to himself before he turns his head, his gaze finally landing on me.

I'm certain he was about to turn and paddle back out, to catch another ride, but instead he lies down on his board and lets the wave take him back in to shore.

To *me*.

His eyes stay on me the entire time, never leaving my face until he's right in front of me, getting to his feet and tucking his board under his arm.

"Nice ride," I say before he can speak.

He smirks. "Thanks."

He undoes his leg rope and throws the cord over his board.

I've always admired that board. It looks just like one my mum had when I was younger.

When I don't say anything else, he walks past me, heading up the beach.

"Jake, wait," I call as I jog to catch up with him.

He looks back at me over his shoulder, his brow cocked in question.

"I couldn't remember if I thanked you... for last night," I say, my cheeks heating. "I'm sorry you had to see all of that... get involved, you know..." I ramble, flustered.

"Don't sweat it, precious. It was no big deal."

I reach for his arm and tug on it, willing him to stop walking away. "Well, it was a big deal for me."

He looks at me hard, and just when I think he might be about to say something genuine, his face transforms into an arrogant smirk. "You're not the first woman to say that after spending the night in my bed."

I narrow my eyes at him in disgust, but in a way, I'm glad he's not treating me any differently than normal.

"You're revolting," I say, barely concealing my grin.

I drop my hand from his arm and settle for walking alongside him up the sand.

"Don't knock it until you've tried it," he quips, that sexy smirk I wish I could hate the way I pretend to, plastered across his face.

"Eden!" I hear a voice bellow, and my stomach drops.

I snap my eyes up at the beach and see Zeke storming towards us, Alexi on his heels and River doing her best to chase them both down.

"Oh shit," I mutter.

Zeke's attention turns from me to Jake and his fists clench tightly at his sides.

"You're dead, Carson," I hear him growl.

"Zeke!" I yell as I scramble forward.

I grab at Jake's arm and try unsuccessfully to drag him behind me.

I hear him chuckle darkly as he takes a step in the direction of my brother.

"Zeke, no!" I scream again as I rush forward, physically throwing myself in the space between the two men.

They're both taller than me, even at five foot ten, they tower over me.

Zeke comes to a screaming stop when he sees me in front of Jake.

He drags his murderous expression from him and lands it on me instead.

"You're trying to *protect* him?" he asks, his voice a mixture of disgust and hurt.

"He's done nothing wrong." I don't know why, but my voice sounds like I'm begging.

Maybe I *am* begging. Begging him to stop. Neither of them need to get in a fight at this point in their careers. Certainly not over me.

Their sponsors will lose the plot if this goes down, because it won't just be a one-punch battle that they can turn a blind eye to – it'll be an all-out brawl.

"Did you or did you not, spend the night in his room, Eden?"

I straighten my spine and look him right in the eye. I've done nothing wrong here. I don't need to apologise for a thing.

"I did. But it's not what you think."

Zeke's expression turns into a sneer. "With that bastard, I'm sure it's *exactly* what I think."

"You have no idea what you're talking about and quite frankly, you're making a fool out of yourself," I say calmly – much calmer than I feel.

"He wants to hit me, precious... let him," Jake taunts him from behind me.

They're both pressing closer together now, and I feel like I'm about to be sandwiched between them.

Alexi tugs on Zeke's shoulder, pulling him back, "Just leave it, man, it's not worth it."

"So, you wouldn't care if it was River he tapped and gapped?"

Alexi makes a growling noise that makes me think he would care. Very much so.

"For fuck's sake, Zeke, I *didn't* sleep with him."

His gaze flickers down to me and he sees the truth in my eyes.

"You lied about where you spent the night."

"I was embarrassed."

I feel Jake step back away from me and I exhale in relief.

"Jake saved her," River pipes up, and I curse her internally.

I shoot her a 'what the fuck' look, and she shrugs in apology.

"I'm done with this shit," Jake announces, stepping around me and brushing past my brother, whose anger seems to have evaporated somewhat, and morphed into confusion. "You still want a fight in an hour, you know where to find me, but trust me, bro, if you're looking for someone to hit, I'd start with the guys that actually did wrong by your sister last night," he calls back over his shoulder.

He walks up the beach, not once looking back at us.

I both love and hate that he's cocky enough not to check if anyone follows.

"You're such an asshole sometimes," I hiss at Zeke as I storm off down the beach, in the opposite direction to Jake.

"Eden!" he calls after me, but he wisely doesn't follow.

"Eden, wait up," I hear River's voice.

"What the hell was that?" I demand as she catches up with me.

"I'm so sorry. We were at breakfast and Zeke thanked Alexi for looking out for you... it just escalated from there. I didn't mean to spill about him saving you... it just slipped out."

I shake my head and sigh in defeat. "Don't apologise. It's not your fault," I tell her as we walk, hopefully far enough away that I won't have to deal with any more drama today.

CHAPTER FIVE

Jake

Fuck.

I don't know why she has to look *so* good.

I guess it's a given with her choice of occupation, but *shit*, she's sinfully sexy.

She's always been gorgeous, but when she first came on tour with Zeke, she was just a baby. Those two years that she disappeared for changed her.

She went from being his kid sister to a sexy-as-hell woman, and I've been drooling over her from a distance ever since. *Fuck*, I think half the guys on the pro circuit have been.

It doesn't help that she's paid to pose in skimpy little bikinis and dresses in front of us twenty-four-seven, either.

She's still a precious little princess though, that much hasn't changed.

There's also the fact that she hates me, but that only makes me want her more.

There's a loud thump on my door and I already know who it'll be.

The bastard has his nose all bent out of shape and he won't let this go until he gets to the bottom of it. He's a good big brother, I'll give him that, but the dude needs to cool his jets. Eden isn't a child anymore.

I stroll, taking my time to answer the door, nothing but a towel wrapped around my waist.

If he decides he wants to hit me now, he's probably going to get a show.

"What do you want, Brady?" I ask him lazily as I pull the door open.

"I want to know why my sister spent the night in your fucking bed," he demands, his eyes darting to my unmade bed before finding their way back to my face.

I could fuck with him right now I realise suddenly. I could make him lose his cool like never before, but I truly just can't be fucked.

I just want to get on the road and onto the next leg of the tour. We're headed for my home town, and I'm homesick as hell.

"She got into some trouble down the beach and you weren't there. She spent the night in my bed, and I slept on the couch. End of."

I go to shut the door in his face, but he shoots his hand out, stopping it from closing.

"What kind of trouble?" he demands, his voice like ice.

"Maybe if you weren't drinking yourself into a coma you would have seen for yourself." I can't help but accuse him.

His expression flashes with disappointment – in himself I'd imagine – before being replaced with frustration.

"I fucked up. Now tell me whose ass I need to kick."

I contemplate my options for a moment, before deciding that I'm happy to throw the guys responsible under the bus. I'll be that guy.

Hell, I wouldn't mind roughing them up myself after what they did to Eden, but I have no right. Zeke, however, does.

"I came in from a surf and I saw a few of the guys, they had Eden lifted up in the air, then they tossed her in the sea."

All the colour drains from his face, which I find interesting given that he knows she's okay. He's seen her this morning with his own two eyes, yet he's still reacting like this is life threatening.

"Shit," he whispers. "What happened after that?"

"I pulled her out. She'd been drinking a bit and she was soaked. She fainted. I carried her back here so I could keep an eye on her. That's all that went on, so relax."

He looks at me like he's confused; frankly I'm confused too. I don't know why I brought her here instead of sending her with River and Alexi, but it was the decision that made the most sense to me at the time, and I've always been an 'in the moment' type of guy.

In fact, it was never really a decision for me; it was just what was happening.

There was no logic to it, having her close defied any.

"Thank you," he grinds out, and I can tell those words taste like acid coming up.

I nod at him. "No sweat." But I've got a feeling he's not done yet.

"I need names."

I smirk at him. "What are you going to give me in return?"

"Don't be a prick, Carson, you know why I need to know."

I nod in appreciation, I *do* know. But that doesn't change the fact that I want something from him in return.

"Tell me why she's afraid of the sea, and I'll tell you who threw her in."

His colour pales again, and I realise I'm scratching the surface of something big here, and for the life of me, I don't know why, but I'm desperate to know what it is.

"She can't swim," he says, but I'm not convinced in the slightest.

"Bullshit."

"Leave it, Jake."

"Alright then." I shrug and go to close the door.

"Wait," he says, his arm hitting the door again with a thud. "It's not my place to say, man, and honestly, it's none of your business."

"It was my business last night when I pulled her from the sea floor."

Zeke flinches, and I almost feel bad for being so blunt.

"Forget it," he says with resignation. "She doesn't need me sharing her business with the world."

He turns and walks away, and it's weird, he didn't give me what I want, but I'm glad about it – I respect him for having her best interests at heart, and not spilling her secrets.

"Joe, Steve and Mark," I call out to him before I shut the door.

***

I get word later that morning that Joe, Steve and Mark got what was coming to them, and I'd be lying if I said it didn't put a smile on my face.

Hopefully Zeke doesn't get thrown off the tour for whatever he did to them; it wouldn't even be a competition without him.

I'm planning to hit the road soon – I'm driving up the coast with a few of the boys then we'll get on a plane and fly out to the town I grew up in.

I can't wait to be home.

I leave my packed bag and my boards in their bags on my bed.

I probably won't be back on this beach until next year, and I want to take one more stroll along the sand. I like to take a minute to appreciate the lifestyle I'm fortunate enough to be able to live.

I get to do something I love every single day and there are not a lot of people on the planet that can say that about their job.

I know it won't last forever, but while it does, I plan to just ride that wave, literally and figuratively. I'll figure the rest out when I'm old and washed up.

Maybe I'll be one of those tanned old dudes that owns a surf shop down by the beach and teaches people how to surf or something.

I look up as I walk, and I can see a bunch of people in the distance.

I swallow deeply. I know what it is, or more to the point, *who* it is.

Eden models for the same surf brand that sponsor me.

Most of the 'baby sisters' club' are just here to watch their brothers and catch some rays, but not Eden, she's here to work too, and as I get closer, fucking *working* it she is.

Jesus, that girl is too hot for her own good.

She's all long legs and killer rack.

Her wavy blonde hair is blowing in the wind, and *damn*, she's so fucking sexy.

Someone yells something out to her, and she jogs over to a makeshift dressing room to change outfits.

I slow my walk so that I'll get to watch her longer, because there's nothing creepy about that.

Nope. Nothing at all.

I swallow deeply as she comes back into view. She's laughing and adjusting her bikini top. I don't know how on earth anyone could swim in that thing, let alone surf, because there's *nothing* to it.

She lowers her hands from the top to tighten the strings on the sides of the bottoms and hell, I swear I get hard. One flick of my wrist and those would be on the floor beneath her.

I'd have her in my arms and on her back before she could even so much as say my name.

"Jake!" a voice calls from behind me, and I realise just how far my dirty thoughts have taken me.

I'm fucking her in my mind for god's sake.

I turn around, my expression hopefully not as guilty as I feel, and my hard-on tucked safely away in my shorts with a bit of luck.

"What's up, man?" I give Max a tip of my chin.

He looks past me to where Eden is back in front of the camera, posing and smiling.

"You're going to get yourself in trouble with that girl. I swear to god, dude, and I'll be there with a big fat fucking 'I told you so.'"

I shrug nonchalantly. "She's fucking hot."

"That she is," he agrees as he pulls his eyes from her, somewhat reluctantly. "But that won't stop her brother kicking your ass."

"For *looking*?" I raise my brow at him and smirk.

He chuckles. "Bro, we both know you're not going to stop at *looking*."

I don't answer, not because he's wrong or right, but because we're within earshot of Eden now, and she'll hate me even more than she already does if she catches me talking about getting into her pants.

She sees us passing by and gives me a small wave and a shy smile. I reply with much of the same, and Max chuckles loudly and smacks my arm.

"You are so fucked."

I scowl at him. "What?"

"You just waved like a ten-year-old girl. You're fucked, bro, just admit it."

I shove him, causing him to stumble a few steps away, still laughing wildly at me.

"She's just some chick that looks good in a bikini," I tell him, and for a minute there, I almost believe it myself.

CHAPTER SIX

Eden

We've only been here two days, and if I thought I was sick of hearing the name Jake Carson before we arrived, I was greatly mistaken.

This is his hometown and the crowds *love* him here.

They've only surfed through one round of heats, but the amount of people that crowded around him when he got back to the beach was *insane*, you'd think they had just handed him the world title right there and then.

"I'm going to *crush* that bastard today," Zeke growls from his spot in the sand next to me.

His heat is up next – he drew a good card. He's up against a bunch of easy beats and Alexi – they should both make it through to the next round without too much trouble.

"If you don't, I will," Alexi replies.

I glance back up at Jake. He's getting his photo taken with a bunch of bikini-clad teenage girls.

I try to resist the urge to roll my eyes but fail miserably. He's such a playboy.

I guess that's what happens when you're hot beyond reason and have the skills to match – women flock to you.

"Why do you and Jake hate each other so much?" I surprise myself by asking Zeke.

I never knew what started this rivalry between the two of them – I assume it began during the years I stayed back home and finished high school, and I've been curious for a while.

I wait until Jake's finished being fawned all over and has turned around to walk back up the beach before looking back to my brother.

"I don't hate him." He shrugs.

"Could have fooled me."

"He's my competition." He shrugs.

"So is Alexi, and you don't want to kill him the same way you want to kill Jake."

"Alexi doesn't want to fuck my baby sister," he mutters under his breath.

"*Excuse me*?" I demand, popping my brow sky high.

"He wants in your pants. Everybody knows it. He's looked at you like a fucking snack... ever since you came back on tour."

"And grew the boobs," Alexi chimes in helpfully.

Zeke shoots him a look that gives the distinct impression that he'll knock his head off if he ever says anything like that again.

"*What*? It's true," Alexi mutters under his breath.

"They are nice boobs." River sighs wistfully. "Wish I had a pair."

"Like fucking hell," Alexi grumbles.

"Can we just back up the truck for a second here," I interrupt them, "you're telling me that you and Jake Carson act like a couple of two-year-olds because you think he wants to have his way with me?"

"I don't *think*, I know."

"You're unbelievable." I shake my head in disbelief.

A guy like Jake would have his eye on one hundred different girls at any one time, even if he *did* like what he saw when he looked at me – which I doubt he does – that's no reason to get into this ridiculous feud.

"It doesn't hurt that he's my biggest competition." Zeke shrugs.

"What am I? Chopped liver?" Alexi scowls.

We both ignore him.

"How about from now on, you just worry a little more about the surfing and a little less about what's going on in my pants, alright?" I say as I get to my feet.

"Not a problem, since there's *nothing* happening in there anyway."

I brush the sand off my ass as I turn to face my big brother, my hands on my hips.

"I'm nearly twenty years old; it might be time you stopped treating me like a little girl."

"Yeah," River agrees, getting to her feet and taking the same stance in front of her own brother. "What she said."

Alexi chuckles. "Yeah, except you're only eighteen. Come back and try again in another two years."

She scowls at him.

I feel bad for River sometimes, but it's hard to have too much sympathy for her when her parents let her follow her brother around on the circuit, *all* expenses paid, with the only condition being that he looks after her and she does what he says.

She has a life most people her age couldn't even dream of. She does her study with a private tutor in the off season and traipses around the globe chasing the sun for the rest of the year.

She could earn her own money like I do – she's been approached so many times to model for various surf brands, but her parents don't approve – in fact they've even gone as far as paying her *not* to pose in front of a camera.

Zeke just looks at me with a smirk. I honestly think he gets some sick sense of pleasure from trying to run my life sometimes.

I turn on my heel, River right behind me, and go to find somewhere else to sit where I won't be under a microscope.

It's just the two of us girls now. Sierra and Jay have gone back home, so we're significantly outnumbered, not that I mind. I'm usually better with boys than I am with girls – River and my couple of other close friends being the exception.

I find a spot on the beach where we'll still get a killer view of the line up and sit down.

There's another surf heat still going, and I watch with interest as two of the guys paddle for position on the wave.

"Do you ever miss it?"

"Huh?" I question River as my eyes stay on the surfer in the blue top – the one who won the race to the wave.

"Surfing... the water... do you ever miss it?"

I shake my head.

"Nope. Never," I lie.

***

"Eden, incoming," River hisses at me.

I twist around to see who she's talking about.

I don't know why, but I'm excited at the prospect of it being Jake, so when my eyes land on Lukah, I'm disappointed.

"Hey, girls," he says as he sits himself down in the sand next to River.

I see her cheeks heat and I make a mental note to find out how long she's been crushing on the baby of the tour.

"Hey, Lukah, bad luck with your heat." I shoot him a smile.

He got knocked out earlier in the day after failing to score a high enough ride to progress to the next round.

He grins. "I got to surf with some of the best out there today. I'm not even disappointed."

That's one thing I like about Lukah. He's not hungry for the win like so many of the guys are – he doesn't care about rank – he just wants to surf and improve. He's getting better on every stop.

"What are you girls doing tonight?" He asks the question as though it's directed at both of us, yet his eyes keep finding their way back to River constantly.

"I dunno." I nudge River's knee. "What are we doing tonight?"

She blushes deeper as his gaze switches to her face. "A few of us were talking about going into town to play pool."

"Can I come?" he asks quickly, and she nods eagerly in response.

I'm so close to squeaking in excitement that she's finally speaking to a guy she clearly likes, when the air shifts around me.

The glaring sun is being blocked, and I'm engulfed in shade.

I turn and glare up at whoever is blocking my vitamin D.

I come face to face with a crotch. A whole different type of D.

My eyes travel further up, and I swallow deeply.

It's Jake. Because *of course* it is.

"Eden." He says my name and I feel it deep inside my body.

"What can I do for you, Jake?" I ask, my tone giving a clear message that I don't really give a shit, regardless of what it is he wants.

"Walk with me," he instructs as he holds out his hand for me to take.

"Mmmm... *no*." I shake my head at him.

"We need to talk."

"We really don't. Now if you don't mind, you're costing me valuable tanning time."

He mutters something incomprehensible.

"Sorry, you'll have to speak up, I don't speak Neanderthal."

He crouches down in front of me, so our faces are only a few inches apart. "I'll tell you what, precious, we're going to talk, and we can do that here, in front of all these people, or we can do it somewhere more private. Your call, brat."

I scrunch my nose up in frustration. He's got me backed into a corner and he knows it.

I'm smart enough to know that a man like Jake means it when he makes a threat like that. He won't hesitate to humiliate me.

"Fine." I scowl.

He smirks at me, and I hate how sexy it is.

He pushes back up to his feet.

I hold my hand out for him to take.

That was my first mistake of *this* leg of the tour.

His hand is so big and warm – it engulfs mine entirely.

He pulls me up with ease, dragging me far closer to him than was in any way necessary.

My boobs brush against his hard chest and he chuckles when I gasp.

He still hasn't let go of my hand.

"C'mon," he commands as he drags me off up the beach.

I shoot River a 'fucking help me' look and the bitch just laughs at me, so I go ahead and make my next mistake – I go with him.

CHAPTER SEVEN

Jake

"I'll have a hot dog and a coke," I tell the chick in the food van. "What do you want?" I raise a brow at a sullen Eden.

She looks at me in surprise. "Nothing. I'm good."

I look her up and down purposefully, even though it pains me to do it without getting a hard-on.

"You need to eat."

She flips me the bird. "I'm just fine, thank you."

"Make it two of each." I turn back to the window and tell the chick serving me, "She doesn't know what's good for her."

"You're in the middle of a competition, don't you think you should be eating a little better?" Eden snaps at me after I've paid and collected our food.

"What's wrong with a hot dog?"

She sets her hands on her hips. "It's processed shit."

I take a bite from the top of one. "It's *delicious* shit. I always eat like this on competition days. Call it a ritual."

I don't miss the way her eyes rake across my bare abdomen. "That's not fair." She pouts. "If I ate like that, I'd have an ass the size of a beach ball."

She's insane. She's a rake. Except for that rack she's sporting.

I shove the hot dog in her direction. "Just eat it, Eden."

She takes it from me, grimacing as she does. "Don't even bother giving me that can of tar – I'm not drinking it."

I chuckle.

I spot a shady area under a tree and start to head for it.

I hold back a chuckle as I watch her nibble on the batter of the hot dog as though it's totally foreign to her.

"Don't tell me you're one of those health freaks."

"You mean one of those people who eat *actual* food, and not this garbage?" She raises her hand. "Guilty."

I chuckle. She really is such a precious little princess.

"Sit," I instruct as I drop to the grass under the shade of the tree.

"Do I look like a dog to you?" she demands as she stands there in front of me in another one of those fucking bikinis, looking the epitome of sexy.

"Sit, stand, I don't care," I say as I crack open my can of coke.

She grumbles to herself before giving in and sitting next to me. "What did you drag me all the way up here for anyway? Better not have been for the terrible cuisine."

I chuckle. She's such a brat.

"Nope," I say as I point to the hot dog in her hand. "Are you going to eat that?"

She shoves it at me. "Not even if I was starving."

I take it and bite the top from it as she watches on in disgust.

"Are you going to give me an answer? I've got better things to do than sit here watching you fill your body with crap."

"I want an explanation for the other night."

I see her tense beside me. "I told you, I'd had too much to drink."

"Bullshit," I drawl as I take the last bite of hot dog.

She watches me chew.

"You *never* have too much to drink."

Her cheeks flush pale pink. "How would *you* know what I do?"

"I've spent a long time pretending not to notice a single thing that you do."

She blushes bright scarlet.

"Plus, you're not some stupid beach ho, Eden, you're smarter than that."

She narrows her eyes at me.

"Plus, big bro wouldn't let you live it down if you did."

She rolls her eyes, and fuck it's childish, but I have to agree with the gesture.

Zeke needs to lay the hell off.

"Why's he always riding your ass?" I ask, trying a different approach.

"*Riding my ass,*" she repeats. "There's a visual I didn't need of my brother. Thanks for that."

I chuckle. "You know what I meant."

"He's just... protective," she says as she adjusts her bikini top, and I must have the self control of a Jedi master, because my eyes stay up, on her face – for the most part at least. "We had a rough few years a while back and he's just taken over the role of my protector, I guess."

I never see her parents around. My mum doesn't make it out often either, but now that I think about it, I can't recall ever seeing Zeke or Eden with anybody that isn't each other.

I want to ask why they don't come out to watch Zeke surf, but the question gets caught in my throat. I've got no right to ask that – I need to stay in my lane if I'm going to get answers from her. I can't push for too much, too soon.

"Why can't you swim?" I ask instead.

"Wha… what?"

"*Swim*, you know." I make a swimming motion with my arms. "Seems like you spend a lot of time around water, you should probably learn."

She hasn't moved an inch, but I can see the panic rising within her.

I should probably feel bad for creating this type of a reaction by pressuring her, but I'm too curious. And I'm an asshole, so there's that.

"I'll keep the idea in mind," she says, her voice nothing more than a whisper.

"Eden, what the hell is going on with you?" I probe, my voice gentler.

I don't know why the hell I care so much but I can't seem to let it go. The desire to know more about her is an urge I can't contain.

"It's nothing, Jake. Okay? I just can't swim. End of story."

The bullshit swirls in the air between us.

"I'm not going to stop asking you, Eden," I tell her, and I'm not sure if it's a warning or a promise.

She narrows her eyes at me. "Well, you're going to be bitterly disappointed."

She gracefully gets to her feet before walking – right on the verge of running – away from me.

I crack open her can of coke as I contemplate what the hell I'm going to do next.

I can't give up. It's just not in my nature.

***

"Stubborn little princess," I grumble to myself as Eden scuttles off down the beach and to the safety of her brother and his girl-friend.

Three fucking days she's avoided me.

It's finals day, which I'm in, *of course*, but for once, I'm not thinking about the waves, I'm thinking about *her* instead, and I'm not happy about it.

I don't know what the hell has got into me; my head has never been this wrapped up in a girl. Not even when I dated Christina Fernandez for six months the summer before last, and *damn* that chick was hot.

Still is actually, but that's not the point.

Eden Brady has gotten under my skin.

I always did like a challenge, and this girl is the biggest challenge I've come across in years.

The worst part about the whole thing is, I can't decide if I'm more intrigued by the prospect of getting into her bikini or the idea of her letting me into her mind.

I'll get her to crack eventually, I know I will. I'm persistent to the point of being obsessive compulsive, and when I want something – I get it.

That's just the way I work.

I watch as Eden says something to Zeke, and he scans the beach – looking for me I presume. I don't know what she's told him, but the fact that I've been chasing her around the beach for days, is probably a good place to start if she wants to get his back up.

I haven't come up against her brother in this leg of the competition, but that's about to change.

We're both in the final, as has become normal – the number one and number two, fighting it out yet again.

She'll have to look at me then.

I throw Zeke a hang loose as he stares at me, and his expression hardens.

I chuckle. His damn sister might be avoiding me, but it would seem that I'm still succeeding in getting under his skin at least.

Always a silver lining.

I turn away to go find my board.

CHAPTER EIGHT

Eden

I release a breath I didn't realise I'd been holding as Jake jogs off up the beach and away from me.

For a minute there I'd thought he was going to follow me over here.

I'm not sure why I'm running from him the way that I clearly am – like a chicken shit – but I can't take his probing.

He's asking questions he has no business asking, and his green eyes seem to see right through the bullshit I've been spewing.

I don't need a man like Jake Carson knowing my business.

In fact, I don't need a man like him for anything at all.

He's arrogant, egotistical and overconfident.

With good reason, my brain reminds me, but I silence the thought.

The last thing I need is my hormones taking the wheel here.

"God, I can't stand that prick," Zeke growls from next to me.

He's watching Jake's retreat up the beach as closely as I am.

Their final is up next, and I feel nervous; not because my brother is going to surf against him yet again, but because I know what's coming.

He's going to do that god damn routine he always does.

The one where he brings his stupid hand up to his stupid mouth and blows me a stupid kiss.

A kiss that I can feel on my lips... from all the way across the fucking beach.

I've considered just disappearing until they're out in the line up and out of view, but I can't seem to do it. Not to Zeke *or* to myself.

I love to hate Jake, and if I give in now and run away, then he wins. And he might be able to beat my brother, but he's not about to beat me.

So instead, I'll stay here and play my part.

"Go get your board and stop plotting ways to kill him," Millie tells Zeke as she gives his shoulder a shove.

He grins down at her and I can physically see the love between the two of them.

They make me sick in all honesty.

They're so deliriously happy with each other.

Zeke leans in as he cups her jaw and kisses her in a way that shouldn't be legal in public.

I turn away. "Get a room," I mumble under my breath.

"I gotta go," Zeke announces.

He places one kiss on the crown of my head and then he's gone, and it's just me and Millie.

"So..." she says, and I already know what's going to follow that one word. "What's going on with you and Jake?"

I give her the side eye. "What makes you think there's *anything* going on?"

She laughs as though the question is a joke.

I raise my brows at her.

"Okay, where do I start..." She holds up her hand to count off the points on her fingers. "There's the fact that you spent the night in his room the other night, there's that little pre-heat routine he's so fond of—"

"That's just to piss off Zeke," I interrupt her.

She ignores me.

"There's also the fact that he's staring at you more often than he's not, and that you blush whenever he's within your sight..."

"I do *not* blush," I argue. "And he's probably plotting ways to make my life miserable."

"He likes you, Eden."

I snort out a laugh. "He does *not*. His only goal is winning, and I'm nothing more than a pawn in his game."

She nods her head and shrugs, her brown hair moving as she does.

"Maybe," she acknowledges as she slips past me. "But did you ever consider the fact that he doesn't need to do *any* of that to win? He's got the talent, hands down, so maybe there's another reason he can't take his eyes off you."

She leaves me with that thought – one that is totally unwelcome in my brain.

I don't know what she's playing at. Zeke would blow his lid if he knew that Millie, of all people, was almost encouraging an interest in his sworn enemy, but I'm pretty sure that that is exactly what just went down.

I know Millie wants to see Zeke back off and let me grow up, but I can't imagine that he'd be accepting of me getting involved with anyone on the surfing scene, let alone the guy he hates the most.

I glance around up the beach and see Zeke and Jake waiting at the water's edge.

They'll get a ride out into the line up and from there; the siren will sound, indicating the start of the heat.

I see the jet skis pulling into the beach and my heart thumps in my chest.

Jake turns, right on cue, and he doesn't even have to hunt for me this time, his eyes find mine immediately and he grins.

I don't know what comes over me, but I smile back at him.

He lifts his arm and blows me a kiss.

I instinctively respond, giving him the middle finger, but instead of my usual scowl, a huge smile graces my face.

I'm enjoying this I realise, this little game we're playing.

There's officially something wrong in my brain.

I watch him chuckle. He dips his head once before taking one final look at me and then running into the water, his board tucked safely under his arm.

"Well that was new." River giggles from next to me. "You know what, I think you like that boy."

I snort out a laugh. "Could you imagine?"

She eyes me sceptically but doesn't say anything more about it as we watch Jake and Zeke surf wave after wave, scoring some of the best waves of the competition. And even though Zeke surfs like he was born to do it, Jake makes beating him look almost effortless.

The crowd goes wild as the final siren sounds, and Jake is announced as the winner, yet again.

I wish I could say I was surprised.

That yellow jersey he's wearing isn't going anywhere anytime soon, if ever.

I watch as Jake rides the wave in to the beach and is hoisted onto the shoulders of his fans and friends.

I can see his coach in there too, patting him on the head as he goes up, his victory being celebrated by his hoards of supporters.

The golden boy with the number seventeen on his back.

CHAPTER NINE

Jake

"Jake, I don't know what to say, you just keep getting better and better. This is your fourth win on the trot; that yellow jersey looks good on you. What does a win on your home break mean to you?"

"There's no place like home." I grin. "But seriously though, a win in my home town is always that much sweeter, and I'm grateful that I got the opportunity to surf here again this year."

"Tell us about the final here today."

"Coming up against Zeke was tough. He always brings his best out there with him into the line-up, and today was no exception, but I wasn't going to give this one up easy, that's for sure." I chuckle.

"Your coach, big wave legend Brad Coles, is there anything he can teach you anymore, or has the student become the master?" he jokes.

"Definitely not." I laugh with him. "I'm always learning from Brad, like you say, he's a legend, and I'm very lucky to have him on my team."

The interviewer claps me on the shoulder. "Well, congratulations again," he turns to the camera, addressing the viewers, "Jake Carson – the winner for this leg of the World Surf League."

The cheers erupt from the fans surrounding me once again.

I might do this for the surfing, but I'd be lying if I said I didn't enjoy this part of the sport all the same.

"Jake!"

I grin as I see Brad walking my eight-year-old brother through the crowd towards me.

"Zayne!" I yell back.

There might be close to twenty years between us, but he's my best friend – even if he drives me insane ninety percent of the time.

He runs up to me, leaving Brad behind and throws his arms around my waist.

"Hey, bud." I chuckle as I wrap my arms around him.

"That was epic!" he says excitedly. "You killed it."

I ruffle his blond hair and he shrugs out of my touch. "Thanks, Z. You wanna go get a milkshake or something?"

He picks up my board for me. "We can go soon. You need to go sign some stuff for your fans."

The kid is seriously my biggest supporter and I wouldn't have it any other way.

"Where's Mum?" I ask Zayne as I take the marker pen Brad is holding out to me.

"She left me with Brad, she had to go to work."

Our mum is a hard worker – she's been a single mum with me and again with Zayne.

She might be a good mother, but she has terrible taste in men.

She refuses to take any of the money I make, so she's still working long hours to provide for her and Zayne.

I scribble my signature on hats, shirts, arms, hell, even fore-heads until I get cramp and my jaw hurts from smiling at people.

Zayne tries to convince me to give away my board to some hot chick about four times, but I refrain.

He's such a little ladies' man.

"Let's get a milkshake already; I'm ready to sit my ass down."

He follows me into the competitors' tent where we ditch my board and wet gear.

We head past the half pipe where a skate competition is still running and into the area where I can get a feed. I'd kill for something greasy right now.

I grin to myself as I think about Eden's disgust over my diet.

"What do you want, Z?"

"I'll take a chocolate shake, fries, and a hot dog."

Unlike Mum, my little brother has no aversion to spending my money.

"Make it two," I tell the guy serving.

I'm leaning against the side of the building, my arms crossed across my chest, when I see her.

Zayne is rambling on, something about one of my rides this afternoon, but I stopped listening about five minutes ago; the kid has verbal diarrhoea.

My eyes follow her as she strolls across the courtyard with River at her side.

At least a dozen heads turn as they walk by, and I can't even blame them.

River might be mostly covered up, but Eden is wearing yet another tiny bikini – this one is bright pink, and she's thrown a pair of the shortest denim shorts I've ever seen over the top.

I bet I could see her ass cheeks out the bottom of those things – not that I'd be complaining.

"Oooooh you're *staring* at her," Zayne announces loudly, causing a handful of people to turn and look at me.

"Shut up," I mutter to him as I attempt to cover his mouth.

He shoves me off and grins. "But you *were* staring. Is she your girlfriend or something?"

"I wasn't staring," I hiss. "Here take your shake and shut your trap." I take the shake from the counter and thrust it in his direction.

If he has something in his mouth, maybe he'll stop embarrassing me.

He grins at me. "You luuuurrrve her."

I narrow my eyes at him. "Take the shake, kid."

He takes it, but he's still grinning like the punk-ass little shit he is.

"Why don't you go talk to her?"

I snag the rest of our order off the counter, handing him his food as I go.

I stalk off in the opposite direction that Eden and River went. The last thing I need is Zayne outing me to her.

He follows, and I swear if he goes for another round of 'Jake and *that girl* sitting in a tree', I might just paddle him out the back of the sets and leave him there.

"Zayne, cut it."

"Go talk to her then," he retorts.

He might be my biggest fan, but he certainly isn't afraid to give me lip.

"Maybe I would, if she wanted to talk to me."

"Why doesn't she want to talk to you?"

"Because I kick her brother's ass all the time." I chuckle. "That's Zeke Brady's sister."

He laughs before taking a drink from his milkshake. "Sucks to be her."

I doubt it sucks to be her at all, but I'm not going down that path, not now that he seems satisfied with my answer.

"Can I stay here with you tonight?" he pleads.

I've been staying at the hotel for convenience while the event was on, but any day now I'll check out and head down the coast to my place for the break.

"If you stop giving me shit about girls," I bargain with him.

"I make no promises."

I shake my head in amusement. He's just like me when I was young.

A total smart ass.

"You should just *make* that girl talk to you," he says after a few moments of silence.

I pop a handful of fries into my mouth. "Oh yeah? You reckon, do you, genius? And how do you propose I do that?"

I spot my sponsors approaching and wave them over.

"I can't come up with all the ideas, Jake," he says with a roll of his eyes. "Go and show up at something she likes or whatever."

I chuckle. This freaking kid.

Bob and Jeff wave back and it's only when I glance at the logo on Bob's hat, that inspiration hits.

CHAPTER TEN

Eden

"I'm sorry, *what*?" I gape at Millie, who is not only my brother's girlfriend, but also my booking agent. (That's how the two of them met – just call me cupid.)

She shrugs, and I can see the mischief dancing in her eyes. "I don't know what to tell you, Eden, that's what I got told."

"It's not fucking happening. She's not posing with that asshole."

That gets my back up, turning my disbelief at the initial request into anger directed at my brother for thinking he gets a say.

"*Excuse me*?" I turn to Zeke, who is sprawled out on the couch. "It's actually nothing to do with you."

"Like hell it's not," he mutters.

"It's my *job*, Zeke, get a grip. You surf with the guy all summer, but I can't do *one* photo shoot? I'm a professional for crying out loud."

"It's actually a series of four shoots," Millie interjects helpfully.

"I don't care if it's four hundred," Zeke drawls lazily. "It's not happening."

I grind my teeth together.

"Well, unfortunately for you, it's not your decision." I turn to Millie. "When's the first one?"

She grins gleefully, and I can't help but feel like she's orchestrated this whole thing perfectly. She knows I can't resist defying Zeke.

"Mills, it's not happening," he insists, turning his argument from me to her.

We both ignore him.

"First one is tomorrow, and the rest are scattered during the break, so you'll have to stay here for the entire duration of the shoot."

"Millie," Zeke barks.

I turn to him, beyond frustrated. I don't particularly want to stay here and work for the next two weeks – especially not with Jake – but I'm damn well going to do it, if for no other reason than to prove to Zeke that it's my decision, not his.

"Look and listen," I snap, clicking my fingers at him. "You might have been running my life for a long time now, and I'm grateful that you've always had my back, but this *isn't* your call. This is my *career*, Zeke, and I'm a grown-ass woman. I'm going to stay here and I'm going to work with him, because it's my *job*."

He sits up a little straighter as though he's shocked that I've finally put him in his place.

"But you'll miss the trip."

Zeke, Millie and a bunch of their friends, including Alexi and River, are all heading to a private island off the coast for the next two weeks. I was meant to be going with them, but that's not going to be happening now, and as much as I want to go, I could use a break from the constant feeling of being watched and controlled.

All the camera crews, fans and crowds will disappear, and this little surf town will go back to its usual charming self. Staying here alone for two weeks won't be much of a strain.

"Well, that's just the way it goes." I shrug.

"But it's your birthday," he replies quietly, and it threatens to crack my resolve.

"It's just a birthday, Zeke, I get one every year. I'll be fine. You can make it up to me next year."

He looks at me with pain in his eyes.

"I'm doing this, and nothing you say will change my mind. I don't need you to agree to anything anymore. I'm an adult, so unless you're going to force me against my will, I'm staying."

He nods his head in resignation. "Fine," he mutters as he gets to his feet. "But if that bastard so much as lays a finger on you, I'll kill him."

"Noted," I breathe as he stalks out the door, even though I'm already one hundred percent certain this photo shoot is going to involve me touching the enemy.

I consider going after my brother but decide against it. He'll get over it, it'll do him good to let go some of his control over me.

"I'll talk to him," Millie promises me. "He'll calm down."

"Thanks," I mutter.

"I think this will be good for you. You never get a break from him." She juts her chin in the direction of the door he just exited.

She's not wrong, but I can't deny the guilt I feel for hurting him. It's just been me and him against the world for so long, and it feels like everything is changing.

"Why all of a sudden do they want me and Jake working together now?" I ask, trying to direct my thoughts into a different direction.

Millie's eyes sparkle. "*He* requested *you* specifically. The label has been on his back for ages about getting a few pictures other than the usual action shots, and he's finally given them the go ahead – on the condition that you were in them too."

Well fuck.

I don't know what to say that.

CHAPTER ELEVEN

Jake

"Jake, Eden, you two know each other, right?" Amber, the photographer asks the both of us.

Eden greeted me this morning with narrowed eyes and a scowl, and I'd be lying if I said I didn't enjoy it.

There's something about her hating me that makes me want to get even closer.

"We've met," Eden answers her sweetly.

"Yeah... we're old friends," I elaborate with a chuckle.

Amber glances between the two of us, sensing the obvious tension. "Well, alright then..."

She's probably trying to figure out why the hell I specifically asked for Eden, when she obviously dislikes me.

"Jake, if you want to go and get into a pair of board shorts, Eden you can get your bikini on, and we'll get started. Maya will help you guys out."

I glance down; I'm already wearing a pair of boardies. Not the *right* pair apparently. This is why I hate this dress-up shit.

I nod at her and head off in the direction she's pointed out.

By the time I get back out, Eden is already dressed and ready to go.

She arrived this morning with her makeup already done, it's minimal and natural – no point in covering up perfection. She looks fucking incredible. Her blonde hair is falling in loose waves over her shoulders, and I have the greatest urge to run my fingers through it.

She's just so fucking tempting.

Her blue eyes are glowing as she watches me walk towards her.

"Alright, let's get the two of you lying together on the beach mat like you're just relaxing at the beach for the afternoon."

We oblige as the camera shutter clicks over and over again.

"Alright, now let's do a few couple shots, if you just get right in close with your faces only a few inches apart."

I can tell by the tense set of Eden's shoulders that she's hating having to do this, but credit where credit's due, she's a total pro and moves in closer to me without questioning Amber.

My hand finds her bare hip without conscious thought and I pull her in flush against my body.

This is exactly how I've wanted her for months now, maybe not right here in front of a camera, but hell, I'll take what I can get at this point.

At least she can't run from me today.

She's so close, I can't focus on anything much but her mouth-watering scent and the warmth of her golden skin.

Thank god Zeke and his little goon gang took off first thing this morning. There's no way he'd be standing by watching this go on if he were here. The dude's probably burst a blood vessel just thinking about it.

"Hey," I whisper as I look into her eyes.

She's so close to me that I could lean in and kiss her if I wanted to, but I won't – I don't particularly feel like getting slapped just now.

"Hey," she whispers back.

We don't say another word as we move through the motions, doing whatever Amber asks us to.

I hold her like she's my girlfriend, and she looks up at me with big, wide, passionate blue eyes.

We play the roles a little too well, even though the tension is still thick between us.

"Get a room!" I hear a voice call.

I breathe out a sigh. "Shit." There goes the peace and quiet.

I glance up at my brother. "Little busy here, bud."

"I can see." He sniggers before making kissy noises.

"Zayne, cut it. I'm working," I warn him.

I hear Eden giggle from next to me as he turns, wraps his arms around his back and pretends he's making out with someone.

"Sorry. That's my brother," I mutter under my breath as I stride towards him.

He takes off down the beach.

"Asshole," I hiss under my breath.

I don't know where the fuck Brad is, he's meant to be watching the little shit for me so I can do this shoot uninterrupted.

I run my hand through my hair in frustration.

"We can take a break if you want," Eden offers from behind me, her tone amused.

"Actually, I need to get a few of Jake alone with the new boards, if you want to take a break, Eden?" Amber suggests.

I feel Eden approaching me from behind. "I can keep him busy if you want?"

I turn to face her, and it's the first time I've seen her smile genuinely all day.

"Ah... I mean that would be great, but you don't have to."

"I don't mind, honestly." She smiles as she shoos me off in the direction of the photographer and lighting team.

"Good luck," I call after her. "He's kind of a handful."

She turns so she's walking backwards, facing me. "I'm yet to find a male I can't keep under control." She smirks, before turning around and strolling down the beach in the direction of my little brother.

"Lucky bastard," I grumble.

CHAPTER TWELVE

Eden

"So why won't you talk to my brother?" Zayne asks me.

My eyes snap from the water, to his face. "What? What do you mean?"

We've been talking for a while now while Jake gets photo after photo taken further down the beach.

"He told me you won't talk to him. He said it's because he's always beating your brother, but I think he was lying."

I hold back a giggle. "What were you talking about me for anyway?"

"He was *staring* at you." He makes a fake gagging motion. "I think he *likes* you." He exaggerates the word 'likes' as though it's the grossest thing he's ever heard.

I can't stop myself from laughing at that. He's obviously still at the age where girls have cooties. He's also delusional if he thinks his brother is interested in anything other than driving me mad.

Clearly the school yard mentality of annoying the girl you like is still alive and well wherever it is Zayne gets his education.

"How old are you anyway?"

"Nearly nine," he announces proudly.

"Wow, that's pretty old."

"Not as old as Jake."

"Not quite." I glance up the beach at Jake as he paddles in the water with the board they've given him to use as the photographer snaps away with the huge camera.

"You like coming out to watch him surf?" I ask.

He practically beams back at me. "Yip. I get to go back to school and tell all my friends that my brother is the best surfer in the world. I'm gonna be the best one day too – Jake says it's in my DNA."

Zayne idolises his big brother; that much is obvious. He's a sweet kid, his smart mouth aside, and I bet he brags about Jake's achievements all the time.

"Do you surf?" he asks me.

"I used to."

"Why don't you do it anymore?"

I swallow deeply. The kid's not afraid to ask the hard questions, even though they're simple ones really.

"I don't really like the water these days."

"Why not?" He's writing his name over and over again in the sand with a stick he found.

"Um, I guess I'm just a little afraid of the ocean."

He glances up at me. "You're too *scared* to go in the water?"

"Yeah." I nod.

"I get scared in the dark sometimes."

I breathe a sigh of relief that he doesn't seem to want more information.

"I think we're all a little afraid of something."

He shakes his head. "Not Jake. He's not scared of anything."

My eyes search the waves for him and find him whipping the board up the face of the wave before dropping down into the white water.

Zayne might be right.

He certainly looks fearless to me.

***

Jake shakes out his hair as he gets closer to us.

"Jaaaake!" Zayne cries, covering his face with his hands. "You're like a dog."

Jake chuckles and ruffles his brother's dry hair.

Zayne shoves him off.

It's really sweet, seeing the way his face has lit up with Zayne around.

"I hope you haven't been giving Eden any trouble?"

He's asking the question to his brother, but he's looking at me, searching my eyes with an intensity that makes me want to shudder.

"He's been no trouble at all."

He huffs out a laugh. "I find that hard to believe."

"I've been an angel, haven't I, Eden?" Zayne smiles sweetly at me, like butter wouldn't melt. That kid is going to be a heart breaker when he grows up – just like I imagine his brother is.

"Hasn't put a foot wrong," I tell Jake.

"See?" He looks up at Jake with an 'I told you so' expression. "Can I go swim now?"

Jake's eyes scan the water, probably looking for rips.

"Just right out here in front." He points out in front of us. "No deeper than your waist."

Zayne has whipped off his t-shirt and is running for the water before Jake has even finished speaking.

I laugh as he bounds into the water.

"He's a really good kid."

He nods in agreement. "Amber said to tell you we're finished up for the day."

"Okay," I say as he takes a seat next to me, his eyes trained on Zayne as he splashes around in the water.

"Why did you do this?" I find the courage to ask him.

"Do what?"

"Request *me* for this shoot."

He glances at me before going back to his watch of Zayne.

"You've been avoiding me. I figured I had to give something a shot."

It makes no sense to me. I don't understand why he cares whether or not I'm speaking to him.

"Well, I'm here now, what do you want?"

"I want you to talk to me."

My stomach is a bundle of nerves. I already know what he's asking. He wants to know about the water.

"Talk to you about *what*?"

"That's far enough, bud," he calls out to Zayne suddenly, and I think that's what convinces me to start talking without any further prying on his behalf.

It's the *love* and care in his voice. He'd do anything for that boy. I can see that. It reminds me of the way Zeke is with me.

"I'm afraid of the ocean. Honestly, it terrifies me."

"Why?"

It was such a long time ago, but it still gives me shivers to think about it.

"My mother died in a surfing accident. I was ten years old. Everyone always used to say that she was part mermaid – like she was born from the sea or something... I guess one day the sea decided to take her back."

I hear his sharp intake of breath. I almost laugh bitterly – that's not even the half of it.

"I was right there, surfing with her. We all were. Me, Zeke and my dad. Her leg rope got caught on the reef and she didn't come up. By the time Dad found her, she was unconscious."

"*Jesus*, Eden."

I can't look at him. I've trained my gaze on Zayne now too. Focusing on him and not the man next to me gives me the courage to keep talking.

"The ambulance came, and they worked on her all the way to the hospital. She was pronounced dead on arrival. She drowned."

"I'm really, really sorry, I can't even imagine."

I wish *I* couldn't imagine. I really do.

I could stop here. I could finish my story now, and it would explain my fear of the ocean without anything further, but it's as though the flood gate has been opened now, and I can't stop.

"We scattered her ashes out at sea. I went in the boat – I'll do that when I absolutely have to, but I've never gone back into the sea... well, not willingly anyway." I laugh humourlessly.

"That's why you panicked. You looked so scared. I knew there was more to it."

There certainly was.

"Those fucking assholes," he growls, and the hatred in his voice surprises me. "They could have killed you."

"So anyway... then it was just me, Zeke and my dad. Dad didn't deal well without Mum. Sometimes he hit the bottle pretty hard, other times he went on surfing trips for weeks at a time, never telling us where he was going, or when he'd be back. Zeke's pretty much raised me since I was ten."

"That explains why he treats you like a kid."

"I guess so. He's been my protector a long time now. He used to put me on the handle bars of his bike and ride me to school." I smile fondly at the memory. "He's a really great big brother."

"I've gotta say, I've got a new-found respect for him after hearing that."

I'm about to call out to Zayne and tell him he's out too far, but Jake beats me to it.

"Zayne, if I see you out that deep again, you're out of there," he warns him. "Don't think I'm not watching."

"Sorry." He smiles at me. "Carry on."

"So, we pretty much carried on like that for a few years, and then one day, Zeke showed up at school in the middle of the day in the old beat-up car of Dad's that only worked half the time... and I just *knew* something was wrong. He was white as a ghost."

I risk a glance at Jake then, and I find his eyes on me, his expression grim.

"It was my dad. He'd gone out for a surf – his board was found floating out back. He'd taken off his leg rope and we never saw him again. In the end we assumed he was dead – held a service and everything. Some people think he got attacked by a shark, others reckon it was a ploy and he just wanted to disappear and start fresh, but I know the truth."

"What's the truth, Eden?" he whispers, as though he's scared to hear the answer.

"He couldn't live without her, so he went to join her."

"You think he did it on purpose?"

I can hear it in his tone that the idea of doing something like that – leaving your two children is inconceivable to him, and I'm glad he feels that way, because I do too – I'm not angry at dad – he did what he felt he had to do, but I'm not sure I'll ever forgive him either, for choosing to leave us when he was all we had.

I nod my head, tears pooling in my eyes. "That's why the water scares me so much. Because I'm worried if I go in there, the two of them will pull me under too."

"Holy shit, Eden," he says, and without another word he wraps his arm around me and tugs me against his firm body.

He just holds me there until I stop shaking and my tears run dry.

I've never broken down in front of someone other than Zeke and River before, and even then, it hasn't been for years.

"I'm so sorry, no one should have to live through something like that."

No one should. But I did. I *have*. So has Zeke.

I pull back away from him, suddenly feeling embarrassed and vulnerable for exposing myself this way.

His arm slips from my back and I hate myself a little bit for feeling disappointed.

I clear my throat. "So, while I avoided the water, Zeke threw himself into it all guns blazing. My dad left us when I was about fifteen years old. By the time I turned sixteen, Zeke had worked his way onto the pro tour and become my legal guardian. He was only twenty-three himself."

"That's pretty cool of him. I remember you being around back then, and then you disappeared. Where did you go?"

My stomach flutters at the fact that he noticed I was gone.

"I went and stayed with my aunty and uncle while I finished high school. Kinda seems like a waste of time now given I pose for photos for a living, but I guess it doesn't hurt to have it completed."

"Education is never a waste of time, Eden."

I know he's right. I won't be young and pretty forever.

I'd love to go to college one day, but I still have no idea what I want to do with my life in the long run. When I was little, I dreamt of being a surfer like my mum, but that's *not* going to happen now, and I've never really found myself a new dream to cling onto.

I can tell he has more he wants to say, but Zayne chooses that moment to run up the beach, shaking his wet hair at us – returning the favour to Jake.

"Hey! What did I ever do to you?" I squeal as he covers me in droplets of cool water.

"Sorry, Eden!" He giggles as he throws his wet body at his brother.

The admiration shining in his eyes reminds me of the way I looked at Zeke when we were growing up – the way I still look at him now for that matter – I owe my brother everything, and that's why I let him get away with so much.

He's earned the right to be a little overbearing – as much as it drives me insane.

"I better get back." I glance up the beach.

I don't know how long we've been sitting here, but everyone from the shoot is packed up and gone.

"Yeah, I've gotta get this little grommet back to Mum's place anyway," Jake tells me.

I get to my feet and brush the sand off me.

"I'll see you tomorrow?" he asks me, his tone gentle.

"You will indeed." I smile at him. "It was nice to meet you, Zayne."

Zayne gives me a wave and a grin.

"Eden," Jake calls after me as I start to walk away.

I turn back and look at him in question.

"Thanks for talking to me."

Butterflies flutter in my stomach again.

"Thanks for listening."

CHAPTER THIRTEEN

Jake

"That was great today, you two – seriously, a much better connection than yesterday. I got some nice shots."

She holds the camera out for me to look, and I can't help but grin as she flicks through a few images.

Eden's on my back in some of them, her grin wide and genuine. There's others of her in my arms, or with her holding my board.

I've had her surrounding me for the past two hours and her scent is all over my skin.

Max was right – I'm so totally fucked.

Looking at her was *never* going to be enough.

I'm not even sure if I like the girl yet, but I want her anyway.

I like her a lot more after getting a glimpse into her past yesterday, that's for sure – she seems a hell of a lot less like a precious little diva after finding out everything that she's been through.

Because *fuck*, she's been to hell and back – Zeke too. I'm not sure I'll have it in me to taunt him after this – the dude lost both of his parents, and virtually became one himself all before his twenty-fifth birthday.

I can't help but admire that.

I don't want to imagine something happening to my mum, but if it did – there's no way that Zayne would be going anywhere other than with me – no matter what changes that would mean for my life and career.

"I like that one." Eden giggles as she points to one of me chasing her down the beach, my board tucked under her arm.

I chuckle. "Smart ass."

I liked shooting that one too. When I caught her, it gave me the perfect opportunity to wrap my arms around her waist and stop her in her tracks.

I also really enjoyed holding her against my bare chest as she squirmed and giggled.

I think I might have enjoyed that too much if I'm being completely honest.

It was a little bit too easy to imagine having her pressed against me in an entirely different setting.

"Let's call it a wrap for today, guys, I want to spend a couple of days editing these shots, and I'll get in touch when I've picked a new location."

She walks off and holds out the camera for her assistant to look at, they both start nodding excitedly as they discuss whatever the hell it is that photographers might discuss.

"C'mon, I'll walk you up." I tip my head in the direction of the beachside hotel that I know she's staying in.

I stayed there too while the comp was on, but I'm checking out today and I'm not sure I've ever been so happy to see the back of a fancy hotel.

My place might not be much, but it's home.

She smiles at me. "You tryna trick me into thinking you're a gentleman?"

I chuckle and shake my head. "Trust me, precious, I'm no gentleman," I say as I reach for her, resting my hand on the small of her back.

I probably shouldn't be touching her, but after having my hands all over her in front of the camera, I'm dying to touch her again when we're away from it.

"Stop calling me precious."

"No can do, sorry."

She mumbles something that sounds a lot like a string of curse words, and I chuckle.

"What are you going to do with your days off?" I ask her, and I'm surprised that I actually care what she's going to say.

She shrugs. "I haven't been to the gym in a while, and I've got a few books lined up to read."

I can't imagine her reading a book; she strikes me as more of a reality-TV kinda girl, but I'm not about to tell her that. I doubt it would go down well.

"What about you?" She looks up at me as she asks, and shit, she's too pretty for words.

I swallow deeply as I try to remember how to form sentences.

"I ah… probably just surfing… be good to be back home for a bit."

We've reached the hotel now, and she stops.

I reluctantly let my hand fall, brushing her ass as it does.

She raises a brow at me, and I chuckle. "Accidental ass brush, I swear." I hold my hands up in surrender.

She giggles and wraps her arms around her bare midriff.

"So, you're not staying here anymore?" she asks.

I'm not sure if I'm delusional or not, but she sounds a little disappointed.

I shake my head. "Nah, I own a place down the coast."

She nods, and I'm definitely not imagining it this time. "Well... thanks for walking me up. I guess I'll see you in a few days?"

She turns, smiles at me over her shoulder and walks towards the door.

"Shit," I mutter to myself.

I don't want to see her in a couple of days.

I want to see her *now*. I'm nowhere near done with her.

"Eden," I call after her, and she stops, turning to look back at me.

"Do you want to see where I live?" I ask as I rub the back of my neck nervously.

I don't know why I'm so on edge, this is far from the first time I've asked a girl to spend time with me, but it's a first with *this* girl.

My breath gets lodged in my chest as I wait for her answer, but when it comes, it's the sweetest sound.

"Yeah, sure."

***

"It smells like feet in here," she says after a few moments.

I chuckle and push the button to make her window roll down so she can get some fresh air.

"I'm not so good with remembering to get wet gear out of the back." I chuckle.

She picks up an empty McDonald's cup from the floor next to her feet and screws up her nose at me.

I snag it from her hand and toss it in the back. "So maybe I'm not any good at cleaning, full stop."

"There's no *maybe* about it."

She should just be grateful that she didn't get in here when we first arrived. I hadn't been inside my four-wheel drive in about three months and smelling like feet would have been a vast improvement.

I probably would have cleaned up for her if I'd thought this invitation through before offering it aloud.

I still don't know what the hell I'm doing.

She's coming to my *house*. Her brother would kill me for this simple act alone, and it would have nothing to do with the fact that I can't do anything other than picture her in my bedroom.

"Is your house as filthy as this car?" she asks, and I can see amusement dancing in her blue eyes.

"I can't go ruining the surprise now, can I?" I smirk as I flick my indicator on to turn left down the narrow road.

She eyes me curiously, but she'll just have to wait and see.

Hopefully she'll be as glad to get away from the hotel as I am.

I feel like I barely slept last night. I had all kinds of crazy dreams, ones involving Eden, Zeke, Zayne and me. My mum was there too, and we were all in the water.

It was bizarre. I don't know how Eden sleeps at all after what she's been through.

Zayne liked her – I could tell. He was all 'Eden this' and 'Eden that' when I drove him home. He told Mum everything about her over dinner and before I left, he patted me on the shoulder and told me that he was glad she finally decided to talk to me.

As far as seals of approval go – she just got the gold star.

Not that I have much of a shot of anything happening between us anyway.

We drive for a few hundred metres more before I turn left again, turning down a gravel driveway that runs parallel with the coast.

She sits up a little straighter and presses the button to put her window down further.

She takes a deep breath of the sea air. For someone who's terrified of the ocean, she sure seems to enjoy watching it from a distance.

"You live right down here?" she asks.

"Yeah. I bought it about a year ago. It's not much, but the location sold me before I even set foot in the house."

We drive up a slight rise, and my place comes into view as we go back down the other side.

"There she is," I announce.

"Wow," she replies quietly.

I pull to a stop near the front door and kill the engine.

She smiles at me, and I don't know who the fuck I think I'm kidding – I need her – no matter how off limits she is.

She climbs out of the SUV and I do the same.

I've got her here now, and I don't have a clue what the fuck to do next.

CHAPTER FOURTEEN

Eden

I'm nervous and I don't like it.

I don't even know what possessed me to get in his big, grey four-wheel drive and come here – but like most of the bad decisions I make, I don't think about the consequences until later.

He's spent the past half an hour showing me the repairs and work he's doing to his house, and what his plans are.

It's incredible – or it will be when he's finished.

To be honest, it could be a steaming pile of shit and I'd still be in love. He's quite literally got the waves on his back-door step. Sand comes right up to the porch.

He lives *on* the freakin' beach.

I don't know why any of this surprises me.

Maybe it's because *he's* surprising me.

He's still cocky and full of himself with his comments, but there's a genuineness there that I'm not accustomed to.

He's touching me all the time too – ever since the shoot this morning, it's as though he can't help himself and I don't know why, but I don't have any desire to make him stop.

He's shown me another side to him these past few days, and I hate how much I like it.

"So, you just live here and surf all day?" I run my hand over the rail of the surf board he's got sitting on a bench in his shed. "What a life."

He doesn't answer my question. "Zayne told me you used to surf."

He moves closer to me, so close that I can feel the warmth radiating from his body onto mine.

"I did," I say with a nod, without turning to look at him.

"I hate that you felt you had to give it up." And there it is again... that genuineness that makes me uneasy.

I shake my head, one small, short movement. "Don't be. I was just a kid. It wasn't my whole life or anything."

"Bullshit," he says, his voice gravelly.

I feel him sweep my long blonde hair over my shoulder so it trails down my back.

I shudder as he runs his fingers down the length of it.

He leans, and I can feel his breath against my ear. "You've got the ocean in your soul, Eden." His shaggy hair is tickling my shoulder and I can feel the goosebumps breaking out on my arms.

I *should* step away.

I should get far, *far* away from this dangerous boy.

I should do *anything* other than tilt my face up over my shoulder to meet his, but instead I do exactly that.

His mouth is right there.

He leans in, teasing me with his closeness, and just when I think he's going to bring his lips to mine, he pulls back a fraction, running the tip of his nose against mine instead.

"Why can't I get you out of my mind, Eden?" he growls.

I shake my head. I can't think of anything but how close he is, and how badly I want him to get even closer.

He turns me around slowly, so my front is pressed against his.

This is dangerous territory, *forbidden* territory even, and I must be a terrible person, because that only makes it more exciting.

I press my hands against his chest which is, as per usual, bare, and revel in the feeling of his warm skin under my palms.

"You make me crazy," I whisper.

"You're so fucking sexy."

His green eyes meet mine and my insides turn to mush along with whatever was left of my resolve.

I shouldn't want this man, but the reality is, I *do*.

I *really* fucking do.

I close the gap between us, rising up on my toes to meet his waiting lips.

I moan as his mouth moulds to mine.

His hands are on my hips in a flash as he kisses me like he's never tasted anything as sweet.

He pulls back, sucks in a few deep breaths and then he's back, his tongue in my mouth and his heart thumping against mine.

I'm on *fire*, and burning has never felt so good.

His strong arms wrap around me and he lifts me onto the bench, right on top of his board.

He pushes his way between my legs, his mouth never leaving mine.

Something so wrong shouldn't feel so right.

He drags my bottom lip between his teeth as I swear, my whole body shudders.

"I've wanted you for so long," he murmurs against my lips, and it sparks a memory in my brain of Zeke telling me that Jake has wanted to get into my pants ever since I came back on the tour.

And here I am handing it to him on a silver platter.

I freeze.

He's kissing my neck and I almost cave, it feels so good.

"Jake," I try to say, but it comes out like a moan rather than a sign for him to stop.

I don't even know when it happened, but his hands are under my singlet top, his fingers brushing my bare skin.

"Jake," I say again, and this time it has the desired effect.

"What's wrong, precious?"

I hate the way he says the name, there's no arrogance there this time, he's not taunting me – it's as though he truly thinks of me as something precious.

I really am deluded.

"We can't do this," I whisper as his eyes search mine.

"Why the hell not?"

"My brother for one... the fact that we don't even like each other is another pretty good reason."

"I mean this in the nicest way possible, precious, but *fuck* your brother. I don't give a shit what he thinks."

"I do," I whisper. "*I* care what he thinks."

Hurt flashes in his eyes, before they harden. "You're going to let him stop you from getting something you want?"

"Who said I wanted you?" I raise my chin in defiance.

He chuckles darkly. "You don't have to say the words aloud to make something fact."

"You just want to get me into bed," I say, and I hate the vulnerability that seeps through in my voice.

He takes one hand from my body and runs it through his hair in frustration.

"I'm not going to lie to you, Eden. I've been thinking about all the ways I could fuck you for a long time now, but I've *never* acted on it... not until now... but after the other night, I can't help myself – you *intrigue* me when I want nothing more than to pretend you don't exist."

I don't know what to say to that. It's compliments wrapped up in insults, and I can't figure out if I should push him away or pull him closer.

My head knows what I should do – *run* – but my body is betraying me, and the butterflies in my stomach are pleading with me to stay.

"I've had a taste now, precious, and I don't want to give you up. You taste too fucking sweet."

"What about Zeke?"

"He's not really my type." He grins wickedly.

I can't help the laugh that falls from my lips. "You're terrible."

"You're so tempting, Eden."

"We need to slow this down," I whisper.

"Whatever you need," he whispers back. "Just stay here with me."

I close my eyes and absorb my own defeat. I already know I won't go. At this point I'm not sure I can. He's not the only one being tempted.

"I'm not going anywhere," I confess.

"Good," he growls. "I'm going to touch you like you're mine, until one day you eventually accept that you are."

"I still don't like you."

"Keep lying to yourself, precious. See how far that gets you."

CHAPTER FIFTEEN

Jake

I've never wanted anything so badly. Hell, I'm not even sure the world title holds as much appeal as she does in this moment, and that's what I've been working towards my entire life.

I've never understood how a woman could make a dude lose focus, but hell, I think I get it now.

She giggles as she looks at the framed pictures hanging on my wall.

"You were *so* cute," she coos. "What happened?"

"I got bigger, and badder." I grab her from behind and she shrieks. "There's nothing *cute* about me now, precious."

She turns and presses her lips against mine, like she can't get enough.

I hoist her into my arms, and there's no way she can miss the hardness in my shorts this time.

She moans and it only makes me harder.

"It's going to be hard to take things slow with you making noises like that," I choke out.

She pulls back and runs her hands through my hair, her eyes glistening deviously.

She wiggles in my arms, effectively grinding herself against me, and I have to take a deep, calming breath to avoid stripping her naked and taking her right here and now.

"Are you planning to take me home any time soon?" she asks innocently.

"Like *fuck*," I growl.

She bites down on her lip, eyes hooded, and I get the impression that my answer pleases her greatly.

"Are you going to feed me at least?" she bargains. "And I don't mean two-minute noodles and a pie, I want *real* food."

"Maybe I'll take you home after all, you're too much effort."

She rolls her eyes. "You know, it wouldn't kill you to eat something that wasn't deep fried... hell, it might even be good for you."

I smirk at her lecture. I wonder how she thinks I've managed to survive this long without her.

"Alright, precious... I'll make you a deal, I'll take you to the supermarket and buy you all the healthy crap you could possibly want, *if* you come and stay with me until we go on the next leg of the tour."

Her eyes widen in surprise, and honestly, I'm as shocked as she is by the suggestion.

I don't even know where it came from, but the longer I think about it, the more I want it to happen.

Fuck want, I *need* it to happen.

I know my time with her is on the clock – that the real world is going to come knocking at any minute, and I don't want to lose a second of whatever *this* is.

"Don't worry about coming on too strong or anything," she says.

I loosen my hold on her and let her legs slide back to the ground.

"I fucking want you, Eden, and not just in my bed, I need you here with me."

She's conflicted, I can tell, and I don't blame her. I've spent the past two years taunting her – winding her up – while really all I've thought about doing is taking her and making her mine.

"Just give me a shot. If you still hate me in a few days, I'll take you back."

Her eyes drift to the door of my bedroom. "You expect me to sleep in there with you?"

"Shit yes I do. I spent one night on the couch while you lay in my sheets, and that's *never* happening again – I can't promise you much, but I can say that for certain."

"Okay," she whispers. The single word floats through the air and settles between us.

She's going to destroy me, this woman, I can feel it. And I'm more than willing to let her; I'll probably destroy her the same way in return.

I'm in over my head here and I'm tired of trying to fight my attraction.

I'll just reach out and take her instead.

***

"I still can't get over how much shit you have," I say with a bewildered shake of my head.

It's *unbelievable*. Considering she spends ninety percent of her time in bikinis and tiny little dresses or shorts, she sure has a fucking huge suitcase.

She bats her long lashes at me and smiles sweetly as she strolls down the supermarket aisle, and she's lucky she's so god damn hot, because this is the worst grocery shop ever.

I thought we'd *never* get past the fruit and vegetables.

I tried to get myself down the potato chip aisle, I really did, but she wasn't having a bar of it.

She's loading meat into the trolley now at least. My job is pushing, her job is selecting what makes the cut apparently.

"Praise the lord, I thought you were going to try and turn me into a vegan or some shit."

She giggles and shakes her head at me.

We add a couple dozen eggs, bread, milk and various other dairy products as we move through the store.

She strolls into the beer area and lifts a dozen Coronas in.

I raise my brows at her. "No chips, but *beer* you'll allow?"

She winks at me. "It's all about balance."

"You're an evil creature. You can't have beer without chips."

"You can, and you will, golden boy."

She skips off towards the checkouts and I make a quick detour while her back is turned. I chuck a can of deodorant into the trolley and just as I'm picking out a box of condoms, she finds me.

She glances at my face, then to the box in my hand.

She blushes but doesn't tell me to put them back.

I toss them in and push the trolley to meet her, tugging her into my side and kissing her head in a gesture that's far sweeter than I thought I was capable of.

"*Jake*, what if someone sees us?" she mutters as she tries to pull away from me.

I tighten my grip. "Sees what?"

"*Us*," she hisses.

I chuckle. "Does it look like I give a fuck? We're here doing a friggin' weekly shop like we're an old married couple or some shit, with a box of rubbers sitting proudly on the top, do you really think I'm worried about being seen with you?"

She blushes deeper red. "Shhh. The whole store doesn't need to know that you think you're going to get into my pants."

"Oh, precious." I smirk. "We both know it's inevitable."

CHAPTER SIXTEEN

Eden

I'm in *trouble*. Like send an SOS, help-me-right-fucking-now kind of trouble.

He *cooks*.... and shirtless at that – because *of course* he does – if I didn't know better, I'd be concerned he was allergic to wearing a shirt at all.

Heaven forbid there was anything genuine for me to dislike about the guy. I'm standing here, clutching at straws as to *why* I should hate him.

He glances at me over his shoulder and smirks at me, his hair falling into his eyes, and I resist the urge to flip him off.

Stupid, sexy bastard.

He knows how good he looks; maybe I'll hate him for that – for flaunting what he's got, even though I'm more than enjoying the private show.

"Are you just going to stand there perving or are you going to help me make dinner?"

"You're doing such a good job, I thought I'd just sit here and look good."

He chuckles. "Sticking with what you know, I guess that's fair."

I take a sip of beer. He shoved a slice of lemon down the neck of it, and the acidity tickles my tongue.

"So... I asked Zeke why the two of you hate each other so much."

He's got his back to me, stirring something on the stove top, and he pauses for a fraction of a second before continuing. "And what did he tell you?"

I shrug. "Nothing really. Just that he didn't appreciate the fact that you wanted to fuck his sister."

He huffs out a laugh. "No, I can't imagine he would."

My cheeks heat. He's made no secret of the fact that he wants me, but it still makes me blush. He's gorgeous, older, more experienced and he wants *me*.

I'm not stupid enough to think that it's about anything more than this pretty little package life has wrapped me up in, but nonetheless, it gives me a thrill.

"So, are you going to tell me the real story?" I probe.

"There is no real story, precious, I'm just good at what I do, and he doesn't particularly like me beating him. Add in the fact that I don't have a problem winding him up, and that I *do* want to bang his sister, and I guess we're just an enemy match made in heaven... but let's be real, it's mainly because I'm better than him." He chuckles.

"You're such a cocky asshole," I say with an amused shake of my head.

"That's why you're so into me."

I roll my eyes at the back of his head. "Oh yeah, I can *barely* control myself when you're around."

He drops the wooden spoon into the pan and turns to face me.

He prowls towards me, and I swallow deeply. "Oh shit," I whisper.

"Oh shit *indeed*," he mutters.

I'm sitting on the bench top, my stool clattering to the ground and my singlet over my head before I can even think 'what the fuck'.

I don't even try to fight it. I might talk a good game, but I'm all shit when it really comes down to it.

I want him so badly I can't think straight.

His mouth is on my skin, dragging kisses over my collarbone, down to my chest.

"I want you so fucking badly, it's causing me physical *pain*," he says, his voice strained.

"Have me," I breathe.

"But you said—"

"I know what I said," I cut him off. "That was *then*, this is *now*."

He won't need to be told twice. I can feel just how much he wants this from the bulge in the front of his shorts.

This might be one of those things that I'm going to regret once it's done, but I'm past fighting it.

I need this cocky surfer boy more than I need my next breath.

He scoops me up and cradles me against his big body.

His lips find the skin on my neck as he carries me towards his bedroom.

"Wait... the food," I say half-heartedly. I don't want to stop, but burning the house down seems like a really bad idea.

"Fuck," he mutters.

He puts me down and turns me to face the direction of his room.

"You've got thirty seconds," he growls in my ear.

He stalks back towards the stove and I bolt towards his bedroom, my heart racing.

I don't know what he wants from me in these thirty seconds; but I want to give it to him.

I look down at my denim shorts and decide they need to go. I'm sure as hell not going to be keeping them on for long if the look in his eyes is anything to go by.

He appears in the doorway as I step out of them, leaving them on the floor.

"That wasn't thirty seconds," I whisper as I take in the expression on his face.

"Jesus, Eden, you're so fucking beautiful."

I have people telling me all the time how pretty I am, or how good my body looks – it sort of goes with the territory of modelling, but I've never, ever felt praise this deeply before.

He walks towards me, each step deliberate and slow as he takes his fill of me.

"I've been wanting to do this for a long god damn time," he growls.

Before I even get the chance to ask what, he reaches out and pulls swiftly on one of the ties on the side of my bikini bottoms.

I gasp, but he doesn't stop, his hand reaching for the other side and repeating the action.

I haven't been with many guys, so the idea of standing in front of an incredibly sexy one that infuriates me, should have me feeling on edge, but it doesn't.

I might live to regret this moment of passion, but right now, I trust him enough to let him carry on.

He steps into me and I wrap my arms around his firm middle.

He's so tight and toned – surfing non-stop will do that to a guy.

I lean in and place kisses across his jaw, all the way up to his ear.

I feel him untie the back of my top, and then the one around my neck is loose too.

I slowly trail my hands down to the top of his board shorts and loosen the tie at the front.

The ripping sound of the Velcro separating is the only noise in the room.

I tug on the side of his shorts and they come loose, sliding down his legs and onto the floor below us.

I swallow the lump in my throat.

Jake Carson is naked in front of me. *I'm* naked in front of *him*.

Jesus what am I doing?

"Don't overthink it," he whispers, interrupting my moment of panic.

I look up into his stunning green eyes, and as he lowers me down onto the top of his bed, I don't think about *anything* but him.

CHAPTER SEVENTEEN

Jake

"Morning," I whisper as I brush the hair from her eyes.

She gives me a small, shy smile. "Hey."

I lean over and kiss her forehead. "How'd you sleep?"

"Like a baby."

There's nothing baby about her. Jesus Christ, the sex appeal on this woman right now; naked in my bed, my sheet curled around her body and her blonde hair splayed across my pillow, I could watch every porn video in the world, and I'd still never get better material than this.

I chuckle as my eyes land on the pile of dishes on the bedside table next to her. We *eventually* got back to the dinner. I wasn't willing to let her out of my bed, so we ate in here.

"Next time we bring food into the bedroom, I'll make sure it's something kinky."

"Promises, promises," she says with a wave of her hand and a cheeky-as-hell grin.

She shrieks as my hand snakes out under the sheet and grasps her hip.

"I never make promises I can't keep," I growl at her.

She's right here underneath me, and if I was ever stupid enough to think that I could fuck her out of my system, then I was an idiot.

A total idiot.

I'm *addicted*.

I'm hooked on everything from her bratty antics to her smart mouth. I'm obsessed with her body from her ass to her eyes.

I'll ruin her, I know that already, but it won't stop me from taking her anyway, because I've got a pretty good idea that she's ruining me too.

"I expected you to have gone surfing already," she says with a yawn. "You haven't been out since yesterday morning, aren't you having withdrawals or something?"

She's a smart girl. I would normally have been up at first light, throwing myself into the cool ocean.

I can't remember the last time my first thought of the morning was something other than hitting the waves, but there's a first time for everything.

This is why dudes say not to get involved with chicks while you're on tour – they fuck with your head.

I can vouch for that – my head's *all* messed up.

"I thought I better wait and tell you where I was going."

"Awww, you're so sweet," she teases. "No one would ever believe me, Jake Carson – being considerate of others."

I chuckle. "Don't you go spreading rumours. It'll fuck with my street cred."

She giggles and I can't help but kiss her. She's so fucking sexy.

Her laughter dies as I brush my lips against hers. I pull back, and her wide, blue eyes are staring right into mine.

"Last night was..." I struggle to find a word that will do the past twelve hours justice.

"Incredible," she whispers.

Even 'incredible' doesn't cover it. That wasn't just sex – it was *mind blowing* sex. It was the kind of sex that raises the bar for all sex that follows.

I nod in agreement as the intensity builds between us.

"I think you should hit the surf," she says, but her eyes are saying otherwise.

I press my lips to hers again. "You trying to get rid of me?" I murmur.

"I'm just warning you," she says with a grin, "if you don't go now, I might not let you leave... *ever*."

"I think I like the sound of that better than surfing anyway," I growl.

She giggles and gives me a light shove on my chest. "Go. Surf before you go completely insane. I don't even know who this man in front of me is anymore, you haven't tried to piss me off for hours and you keep saying sweet, *charming* things..."

I chuckle. "Alright, alright... What are you going to do?"

"I might go for a run."

"Practising your get away for when I turn back into the ass-hole you know and love?"

"Something like that." She giggles.

***

I look back into shore over the backs of the crashing waves. She's still sitting there, reading some book. She's been there for over an hour, twirling her hair around her finger, reading or just watching me.

She's seen me surf hundreds of times, and I've competed in front of some of the most critical judges in the world, but I've *never* felt like this. I can feel her eyes on my every move.

I wish I could bring her out here.

The ocean is my home and I want to share it with her.

I groan and shake my head at myself. This isn't me.

I'm not the guy who pines after a woman. Especially not one like Eden Brady.

I slap the water with my hand.

I'm screwed. She's invaded my head, and it doesn't matter what I try to tell myself, it's *too late*. I've let her in and there's not one part of me that wants her to leave.

She's staying in my house for crying out loud, and I hate the fact that it's the highlight of my year.

I suck in a deep breath of salty air and exhale slowly.

I've wanted Eden for years, and I've finally got her.

I need to forget about rules and boundaries. I need to forget about her brother and the competition, and just think about me and her, and all the things we can do together that won't feel wrong at all.

I take another breath and it calms me this time.

I glance out back and see a big set coming in. I pick my wave and grin as I feel the familiar push and pull of the ocean beneath my board.

She was right. I needed this.

I surf until I'm back to the man I remember, the one who would never give up on something he wants.

I land my eyes on the stunning blonde sitting on the sand waiting for me as I lie down on my board and let the white water take me all the way in.

"Feel better?" she calls as I approach.

My face breaks out into a big grin. "Sure do, precious."

She smirks at me. "It pains me to say it, golden boy, but you looked good out there."

"Oh yeah?" I chuckle as I drop my board on the sand next to her. "Watching me on a board get your motor running, does it?"

"Brrrmm, brrrmm," she replies dryly.

I drop to my knees in the sand. I'm drenched, and she's being a smart ass – it's not going to end well for her.

"Don't even think about it!" she shrieks as I lunge for her, knocking her back onto the warm beach.

"C'mon, precious, it's just a bit of water."

My hair falls forward and drips salty water onto her face.

"Get off," she cries, while shoving at me, a huge smile on her face.

I smack my lips on hers and pull back, dragging her up with me.

She makes a show of shaking herself off.

"You're such a princess." I chuckle.

She shoves me again and I nearly topple over to the side. "Fiesty." I smirk.

We sit next to each other, both of us watching as the water laps at the shore.

When I turn to look at her, she's looking at the sea with what looks like longing mixed with fear.

I *hate* that she feels this way.

I'd give anything to take away her pain.

I reach for her hand. "Do you trust me, Eden?"

She looks at me then, and I don't doubt her when she answers, "yes."

CHAPTER EIGHTEEN

Eden

He gets to his feet and pulls me up with him.

"Where are we going?" I ask.

He starts walking towards the sea, towing me along beside him.

"*Jake*..." I say warily.

He turns back and looks at me with such tenderness my heart melts. "Just trust me, Eden, okay? You can trust me. I promise."

I nod, even though I feel like I'm going to cry because I already know what he's asking of me... *why* he wants me to trust him.

He leads me into ankle-deep water.

He turns to face me, placing a hand on each of my shoulders. "This is okay, right?" he asks as he ducks his head to bring our eyes level.

I bite down on my bottom lip and nod my head. He noticed – that I only ever get my feet wet and no more. He really does pay attention to the little things about me.

"Let's take another step."

I feel my eyes widen.

"You can show me vulnerability, Eden... you don't always have to act so tough." He cups my face, and I melt.

"I'm scared," I admit.

"I'm not going to let anything happen to you, precious, I'm right here. I won't let go of you, even for a second."

I'm *terrified*, but I believe him. I trust him – as stupid as that might make me – but I know he won't let anything happen to me.

I've avoided the water for years, but I've never had him. I've never had anyone *try*.

Zeke never wanted to push me, so he just accepted that I'd stay out of the water until I was ready. And while I appreciate him respecting my choice, it would have meant a lot to me if he took the time to try and help me overcome my fears even once over all these years.

Exactly the way Jake is now.

I know he wants to help, and as shit scared as I am, I don't want to be afraid anymore.

I nod my head at him. He hasn't moved a muscle – he's been waiting for my permission and I love that about him in this moment. He's making sure I know this is entirely my choice.

He takes one step deeper and I follow.

The water laps at my calves. I breathe deep – it's not so bad.

"Another one?" he asks gently.

I look right into his eyes and find the courage to nod again.

This time the water is up to my knees.

I try to ignore the feeling of it pulling on me as the waves wash back out to sea.

"Jake..." I whisper. "It's tugging at my legs."

"Embrace it, Eden, you're safe. I'm right here, *look* at me."

I realise my eyes are squeezed shut.

I slowly open them and look back into his sure green eyes.

"You're doing so good, baby, I'm *so* proud of you."

Butterflies flutter in my stomach as he praises me, and for a moment I forget where I am, all I can think about is him.

He steps back again, and I squeeze tighter on his biceps. I'm in nearly up to my ass now.

"I need you to hold me," I whisper, and there's a shake in my voice – one that is quickly finding its way into my limbs.

His arms wrap around me tightly, and we stand there like that until I feel my tense muscles relax.

He's so patient. He doesn't once push me to go further than I'm ready to venture.

"You're *incredible*, Eden," he says, his voice muffled against my hair. "We can go back in now if you want?"

I shake my head. "I want you to carry me out further." I'm terrified, but if I can't do this now, here with him, I might never find the strength.

He pulls back, just slightly so he can search my face. "You'd trust *me* to do that?"

My heart thumps in my chest at the pride in his voice.

I nod again.

I'm not sure I can speak any more. I'm freaking out, but I need to do this. Right here – with *him*.

He scoops me up into his arms, and I lock my legs around his hips like a vice.

My arms are wrapped so tightly around his neck, it must be uncomfortable, but he doesn't complain once as he slowly strides into deeper water.

"The minute you want to go back, you tell me, okay?"

"Keep going," I whisper.

I close my eyes tight and try to focus on the warmth of his skin, the way his hair tickles at my shoulder and the clean scent of his skin.

"Eden," he whispers. "Open your eyes, precious."

I take a deep breath and open them, I peek out over his shoulder and I can't believe where I am.

I'm in the water. *Deep* in the water.

The cool ocean is lapping at our shoulders as he holds me flush against his body.

"You did it."

Almost hysterical laughter bubbles up my throat.

It's been nearly ten years since I've experienced this, and I don't know whether to laugh or cry at the fact that it was *him,* of all people, that I trusted enough to make it happen.

The world works in mysterious freakin' ways.

"Are you okay?" he asks as he nuzzles at my neck.

I don't know how, but I *am* okay. His strong arms are holding me tight, and I trust that he won't let anything bad happen to me.

He's got me.

"Thank you," I whisper as I feel tears building in my eyes. "I don't know what to say."

"You don't have to say anything," he replies as he kisses my forehead.

I don't know what to make of the trust I've placed in him, but I can't deny that this moment has changed something between us.

We stay there like that for what feels like forever, until he decides that I've conquered quite enough fears for one day.

He carries me all the way back to the house, his board and my book abandoned on the beach, and right back into his room, a look in his eyes so intense it's impossible to look away.

I can feel myself falling for him – *the enemy*, and even though I can think of a million reasons why this is a bad idea, as long as he's looking at me like that, I'll ignore every single one of them.

CHAPTER NINETEEN

Jake

Every day she gets a little bit braver.

Earlier today, she walked out until the water was up past her waist, only holding my hand for support.

I'm so fucking proud of her.

I saw that terrified look in her eyes when the guys tossed her in the sea that night – hell, I pulled her from the ocean floor myself because her own fear was so paralysing that she couldn't even save herself – so this is a massive accomplishment for her.

I'm proud of me too – that she's got enough faith in me to trust me with something so damn important.

She's literally putting her life in my hands.

I'm that guy for her. I'm somewhere she feels safe.

Who the fuck would have thought?

Zeke is going to kill me – Alexi and the other guys will help him – hell, Max will probably even get in on it since he warned me it was a bad idea, but I don't give a shit. If it means I get to have her then I'll go to hell and back to make it happen.

I can handle a few surfers throwing punches.

I'm not giving her back. No way in hell. I've had a taste now – of her trust, her body and her mind... that little princess is *mine*.

"God, you are something else," I growl as I stand at arm's length away from her in the knee-deep water.

She grins at me, her whole face shining with happiness.

I so badly want to grab her and hold her close, but this right here is about her, not me – and there will be plenty of time for that later – that's the beauty of holding her captive here all by ourselves.

I'm even starting to enjoy the healthy food she's forcing me to eat.

She's got me completely brainwashed, and I couldn't be happier about it.

She walks out a little farther and I can see her nerves starting to get to work.

"Talk to me," she says.

"What do you want me to talk about?" I ask as I walk alongside her, watching her face carefully, looking for any sign that she might panic.

"Anything... tell me about when you started surfing."

I chuckle. "I can't think of a time when I *didn't* surf. I grew up next door to Brad Coles – my coach. My dad took off when I was little, so Brad kind of adopted me when he was around."

"I didn't know that," she replies as she takes smaller steps forward. "That's really sweet of him."

"The guy's a legend."

"So, he's always been your coach then?"

I shrug. "I guess so. He moved away when I was about ten or eleven, but he came back all the time and he taught me everything I know. He was always there cheering for me at competitions and stuff... I'm pretty sure he even paid for some of my entry fees when Mum was short on cash."

"I like that." She smiles.

"You like what?"

"That he had your back – that he still does... I like learning about where you came from. It's nice to hear the story of you." She grins wickedly. "Makes you seem like a little bit less of a douche."

I shake my head at her and smirk. "Glad to hear it, precious."

We're nearly up to her armpits now; this is the farthest she's ever ventured without being wrapped around me like ivy.

I don't even want to say anything in case it spooks her, but holy shit, I'm impressed.

"Why do you wear a seventeen on your jersey?"

She knows that everyone in the surf league gets to choose their own number for their jersey, and sure, some just pick random digits, but for most of us, there's a reason for the one we choose.

"I was seventeen when Zayne was born – changed my life forever, becoming a big brother – so it's for him."

"Jesus, Jake," she chokes out, and I reach for her in a flash, but she's smiling, not panicking. "Are you trying to make me fall in love with you or something? That's the sweetest thing I've ever heard."

I chuckle.

"I need to get back to land..." She fans her face dramatically with her free hand. "Being a brother *changed your life*... holy shit my ovaries might just combust on the spot." She shakes her head in disbelief as she wades back into shore, the waves crashing against her long, sexy legs, like it's no big deal at all.

I wait until she's back in shallow enough to feel comfortable before grabbing her and tossing her over my shoulder.

"You think you're *so* funny." I chuckle as I swat her ass as she giggles and shrieks.

"That's because I *am* funny."

I throw her down onto the sand, making sure that she lands softly.

I start tickling her and she shrieks louder.

"Sorry, precious, no one can hear your cries for help out here."

The nearest house is so far down the beach I can't even see it.

"Stop! I'm going to pee myself!" she cries as she tries desperately to escape me.

"Better tell me something good then, before you wet those sexy little bikini bottoms."

"What... do... you... want?" she chokes out between giggles.

"I want information, precious, and *you're* going to give it to me."

I continue tickling as she gasps for breath through her laughter.

"You're pure... *evil.*" She giggles.

"Sorry, sweetheart, that's not a winner. Try again." I smirk.

She laughs louder as I find a secret spot on her side.

"Fine, today is my birthday!" She squirms out from under me as I stop tickling. "Holy shit, I swear I nearly did pee a little bit."

"You're fucking with me, right?" I demand.

She narrows her eyes at me. "I didn't *actually* pee, relax."

I huff out a laugh. "Not *that*, you little fruit cake, the birthday part... is today seriously your birthday?"

She nods shyly. "Sure is."

"Why the fuck didn't you tell me?"

She shrugs. "Never came up... and I didn't want to make a fuss."

"How old are you?"

I feel like I should already know this piece of information given how many times I've been inside her these past few days, but like the jackass I am, I never thought to ask.

"Twenty today." She smiles sweetly.

I can't fucking believe this. It's her god damn birthday and she's here with *me* – an idiot who had no idea.

It's bad enough she doesn't have her mum or dad around to celebrate with her, but because of me and my demands that she do this shoot, she's not with her brother or her friends either.

I'm a class-A wanker.

"Right," I announce. "Go get dressed. I'm taking you out."

I pull her up to her feet and she sets her hands on her hips like a brat.

"And what if I don't want to go out?" She pops a brow at me.

"Well bad fucking luck, precious, it's your birthday and I'm the best you've got today, and I'll be damned if I'm not going to take you out."

I turn her around by the shoulders and march her in the direction of my back porch.

"You're so bossy," she says, and I'd be willing to bet my house on the fact that she just rolled her eyes.

"Just get that sexy fucking ass into some clothes and don't argue with me for once in your life."

"But where's the fun in that?" She turns and smirks at me before skipping off in the direction of my bedroom.

I chuckle. She's right – the fight is half the fun.

I slap her ass as she darts away from me.

"You're not taking me to McDonald's, are you?" she calls warily from inside my room.

Shit.

Not anymore, I'm not.

"Nope. I'm taking you somewhere even better," I reply.

I run my hand through my hair in a moment of panic.

What the fuck do I do now?

***

"Where are you taking me?" She giggles as she looks out the window for clues.

We passed the McDonald's about five minutes ago and I had a little bit too much fun pretending to turn in there and almost got us into a car crash.

I've never seen her laugh so hard.

Then I made her sit in the car while I ran into the supermarket to buy her a cake that probably tastes like shit and a packet of two-dollar candles to stick in the top.

She pretended not to notice me carrying it out, but the twitch in the corner of her mouth gave her away.

I pull up on the side of the street and kill the engine.

I lean over her and glance at the house.

I hope this is okay.

I really should have asked her first. I run my hand through my hair nervously.

Shit... what if I've got it wrong? Spending time with *my* family might upset her given that *hers* isn't around.

"What's with the frown, golden boy?" She rubs her finger at the crease between my eyes.

"I'm not sure this is such a great idea after all."

"What is it?" she probes softly. "It can't be worse than fast food, right?"

It's not the food I'm worried about, my mum will have plenty of it, and it'll be delicious, even with no notice, she always seems to cater for a small army.

"I shouldn't have assumed... I just figured you must miss your parents on days like today..." I shake my head at myself. I'm an idiot sometimes. "I thought you might want to spend your birthday with my family... it was probably stupid... we can do something else."

"Jake." She laughs softly and grips my arm. "I'd *love* to have dinner with your family."

"You would?" I breathe a sigh of relief.

She cups my jaw with her hand. "You are so sweet when you're nervous."

Her lips brush mine, and I relax. She's not upset. If anything, she seems excited.

"I have something for you," I tell her as I kiss her softly one more time.

"Oh yeah, and what's that?"

I pull away from her and reach into the glove box. I pull out the small fabric bag from where I shoved it before she got in the car.

"It's not much... but I thought you might like it."

I watch as she loosens the strings on the bag and tips the pendant and leather cord out into her palm.

She flips it over in her hand.

"It's beautiful," she breathes. "What is it?"

"It's sea glass," I explain as I hold my hand out for it and hold it up to show her. "I found it on the beach a few days ago and I thought you might like it."

"It's the colour of the ocean."

"When I was little, I used to find them for my mum. She always called them ocean treasures and said they were gifts from the sea... when I saw it, I thought of you."

She looks into my eyes and I see tears welling in the corner of hers.

"If you don't like it, you don't have to wear it."

She snatches it from my hand and slips it over her head, all the while scowling at me. "I love it, you stupid fool." She wipes at the tears that are threatening to roll down her cheeks. "It's beautiful, thank you, Jake, I love it."

"Happy birthday, precious," I whisper as I kiss her again.

CHAPTER TWENTY

Eden

"I can't believe you didn't make this beautiful young woman a cake for her birthday."

I hold back a giggle at the bewildered expression on Jake's face.

When he said he was taking me out, I never imagined I'd be meeting his mum and hanging out with his brother again, but I couldn't have asked for better.

I haven't had a family dinner in a long time.

"In my defence, Ma, she kept her birthday a secret from me, and you're eating some of her cake right now."

She points her cake fork at her son. "But you didn't make it yourself now, did you? This is a *store bought* cake."

"Jesus Christ," he mutters under his breath, and this time I do giggle.

He pulls his cell phone from his pocket and taps away at the screen. "There," he announces. "I've got it locked into my calendar so I can make sure I bake her a damn cake next year."

My heart rate accelerates in my chest at the thought of him making plans a year from now – even if it is just to shut his mother up.

He winks at me, and I smile nervously in return.

"So, tell me more about these shoots you two have been doing," she prompts as she takes another mouthful of cake. Considering she wasn't happy about it being store bought, she sure seems to be shovelling it in.

Jake's smile widens as he glances at me.

"The crew came out to my place and we did two more shoots on the beach," he tells her.

I feel myself blush. I don't know if couples shots were really the way the shoot was intended to go, but that's sure how it ended up. My blush only deepens when I think about what we got up to on that same beach after the photographers left.

"So, do you have any more lined up?" she asks.

I shake my head. "They said they had more than enough material." I shrug, and squeeze Jake's leg under the table knowingly.

"I'm just that good." He puffs out his chest, and I roll my eyes.

Zayne laughs, slapping his hand over his mouth to try and hide it, and I grin at him.

"He's really *not* that good," I say in a stage whisper.

He laughs again. "I bet they made you *kiss* and hold hands." He shudders at the mere thought of all that disgustingness.

Jake shakes his head in amusement and lightly punches Zayne's arm. "They sure did. I'm covered in girl cooties, bro."

"Ewwwww." Zayne grimaces. "That's gross."

"*I'm* gross?" I ask him with raised brows, fake outrage thick in my tone.

He winces. "Sorry, Eden, it's not your fault you're a girl."

We all laugh.

Jake leans in, his mouth brushing my ear. "Just for the record, I really like your particular cooties. And I *especially* like the ones that live in your p—"

I squeeze his leg to stop him from talking and he chuckles.

I blush as he straightens up, his mother and brother none the wiser to his filthy mouth.

"Seriously though, Ma, you should see Eden's pictures, she's made for it."

She smiles sweetly at me as I blush again. "Now *that* I believe."

She's such a lovely woman, I don't know how she managed to raise such a full-of-himself, punk-ass son, but deep down I see a lot of her in him.

He's sweet, compassionate and protective underneath all that bravado.

It's just a matter of stripping his ego back, one layer at a time.

"Jake and Eden sitting in a tree, K-I-S-S-I-N-G," Zayne bellows before Jake slaps a hand across his mouth.

"fwisrt cowmes lowve," he murmurs, trying to sing through his brothers hold.

"That's it, kid, you're out of here," Jake announces as he scoops Zayne up and tosses him easily over his shoulder.

I giggle as he walks him out of the room, stopping only to wink at me before disappearing.

"Kids." She shrugs with a laugh. "You gotta love 'em."

I giggle. "I think he's pretty great."

She looks at me curiously, her expression probing but soft – it's a real 'I'm a mum and we need to have a boy chat' face. "Are we still talking about Zayne?"

She doesn't look old enough to be Jake's mother, so she must have had him young.

I blush and dip my head.

"That's what I thought." She smiles. "He's a good boy when he's not strutting around like a peacock."

I giggle. She knows her son well.

"Have you known each other long?"

I don't really know how to answer that. I can't exactly tell her that we've been hurling insults at each other for the better part of the last two years.

"My brother is on the tour too," I say by way of explanation.

"Ah." She smiles knowingly. "Which one is he?"

"Zeke Brady?" I offer.

Her eyes widen. "Well now... you *have* found yourself in quite the pickle then, haven't you?"

I giggle nervously. "I'm not sure I know what you mean..."

She raises one of her dark brows at me. "You don't fool me, sweetie, I know all about those boys and their rules *and* their nonsense. I've been a surf mum a long time now, even if he thinks he's all grown up these days."

Busted.

"My brother doesn't know anything about me and Jake," I admit.

I don't know how I've found myself in this position, having a D and M with the guy I'm sleeping with's mother, but here I freakin' am. It's as though I'm a magnet for awkward conversations these days.

"I might not have had a date in years, and this might be terrible advice, but you and Jake seem happy – if you think your brother is going to ruin that for you, then you shouldn't feel like you have to tell him – not until you're sure there's really something there to be ruined. Do you know what I mean?"

I think that makes sense. I don't even know if Jake is serious about me, or if he'll want anything to do with me once we go back to reality.

I need to figure that out before I worry about telling Zeke *anything*.

"See how it goes for a while. Worry about the rest later, honey," she encourages.

"Thanks." I smile at her.

"But just so you know, I haven't seen my Jacob look so happy in a long time." She giggles. "Well, I mean, he's always happy – mostly with himself," she says with a roll of her eyes. "But he's never been this happy *with* someone."

I don't know what to say to that.

"Boy's his own harshest critic and biggest fan. Never seen anything like it," she muses.

Jake chooses that moment to come strolling back into the room.

"I told the little turd to hit the showers." He chuckles before looking between his mother and me. "Uh oh. Why do I get the feeling you're about two seconds away from bringing out the baby albums?"

"Ooooh, can we please?" I beg.

Jake says, "No!" at the same moment his mother says, "Of course we can."

I giggle.

"This is why I don't bring girls here, Ma," Jake says with a grin and a shake of his head. "You have absolutely no ability to keep my shit personal."

She waves her hand at him dismissively and I watch his eyes soften as he looks at her.

He loves his mum. It's the most obvious thing in the world.

"Alright, birthday girl, it's time to go before she gets the chance to ruin my reputation."

"Oh." I pout. "But I was really looking forward to seeing embarrassing pictures of you," I tease as I get to my feet.

"Next time, I promise." He chuckles as he drags me into his side and wraps his arm around my middle.

I don't know if I'm being hugged or held hostage.

"Fine." I pout again like the diva I am, but on the inside, I've got butterflies about him promising that he'll bring me back here.

He's nothing I expected, and *everything* I expected at the same time.

I don't know what we're going to do in four days' time when everyone meets at the next stop on the tour.

This desire he has isn't waning, neither is mine, not in the least.

I'm not sure I can go back to the way things were, and what's more, I'm not sure I want to. But this – whatever this is, is undoubtedly about to get a hell of a lot more complicated.

***

I'm standing in the armpit-deep water, and Jake is floating lazily on his back a few metres away.

I'm doing it.

I'm really fucking doing it.

It took me another couple of days, but now that I'm out here, I'm not so scared anymore.

He has somehow managed to erase my fears almost entirely.

I look out at the horizon and take a deep breath, clutching the sea glass pendant he made for me before gently pushing my arms under the water, diving, followed by my head and body.

I keep my eyes squeezed shut and pop back up quickly.

"Ha!" I yell with a grin as I take a breath of fresh air.

It's exhilarating. I can see why Zeke loves it so much out here. I feel I'm giving my fear of the ocean the middle finger – as though I'm telling it a giant *fuck you*. It may have taken my parents, but it's not getting me.

I look over to where Jake was floating, expecting him to still be there, but he's not. He's right next to me, and the look on his face is one of pure admiration.

"You went under."

I nod at him excitedly.

I kind of feel like a little kid at their first swimming lesson, but I don't care. This is big for me – huge even – and I owe it all to him.

I lunge for him, throwing my drenched body against his.

He catches me effortlessly and holds me tight.

"I would never have *ever* been able to do that without you," I tell him as he lowers us into deeper water.

"It's all you, precious, trust me."

"I *do* trust you, that's the reason I'm in the water right now, Jake."

He dips his head, my praise clearly making him feel uncomfortable.

"Don't go turning all modest on me now, golden boy," I tease.

"*Me*, modest?" He smirks.

I resist the urge to roll my eyes. "I think your fearlessness has rubbed off on me," I say with a content sigh.

"What makes you think I'm fearless?" he asks, his eyes searching mine as he holds me close.

"Zayne seems to think you're not scared of anything, and I have to agree. I've seen the way you do life, Jake – nothing holds you back... you're not afraid of a single thing."

"I'm afraid of losing you," he whispers, his tone vulnerable.

My heart races and my insides turn to mush. I'm this strong, daring man's weakness, and the idea of that does crazy things to my heart.

It also answers my questions – this is real for him too.

"I don't want to go back, precious."

I know what he means.

Tomorrow we get on a plane and leave this little piece of paradise behind.

We'll have eyes on us from every angle when we get to the final stop on the tour – the one where I have no doubt that Jake will be crowned the winner of the world title.

I don't know what the fuck we're going to do.

We've barely talked about it; instead I think we're both trying to pretend it's not happening.

But time is nearly up; we can't put this off any longer.

"We'll think of something," I say and it comes out like a promise. "If you want to?"

I don't even know what we are – if we're anything at all. This whole thing has become so complex. This isn't a simple boy meets girl.

"You're *mine*, Eden. That's the only thing I'm sure of."

My heart races. Belonging to someone never felt so good.

"What do you want to do about Zeke?" he asks quietly.

I place a kiss on his cheek. "For now, I think we should keep this between us, and we'll worry about Zeke when we're ready. I might decide you're a cocky prick once we get back to the real world." I giggle.

I feel his fingers stroking my skin under the water. "Oh, precious, there's no doubt about it." He smirks that arrogant smirk that I love to hate and then chuckles.

I wrap my arms around his neck and pull him in close. I can feel tears prickling in the corners of my eyes.

I don't want to lose him now that I know what it's like to have him.

"We'll figure it out, Eden. I promise," he says as he holds me tight.

CHAPTER TWENTY-ONE

Jake

I've never hated being on location so god damn much. I've never hated being on a beach with waves crashing at my feet ever, actually... but this sucks a bag of friggin' dicks.

I can't touch her.

I can't kiss her.

I can barely even fucking look at her without drawing unwanted attention.

The competition starts tomorrow, and I already can't wait for it to be over.

This is quite possibly the highlighting moment of my career, and I'm not even bothered right now.

I'm completely screwed.

I've fallen in love with a bratty, precious little princess and I'm over the god damn moon about it.

I fucking love her and her sexy god damn ass.

She's nothing that I thought I wanted in a woman and that only makes it more appealing, forbidden fruit and all that shit, I guess.

I am grateful for one thing at least – word on the beach is that River hooked up with Lukah while they were away, and that means everyone is gossiping about that, and not the fact that me and Eden stayed behind together.

Alexi is bound to rough the poor little bastard up when he finds out, and he *will* find out – I don't know how he hasn't heard already – so maybe Alexi will be too preoccupied taking care of his own sister to worry about helping Zeke kick my ass.

That's the least of my concerns right now anyway.

My main problem – a really fucking big problem if you ask me – is finding a minute to get my hands on my girl.

A few flirty smiles and one stolen kiss are not cutting the mustard.

We're having a bonfire on the beach later on to celebrate this being the final leg, and if I don't get an opportunity to steal her away tonight then I never will.

"You're staring again," Max states as he bumps his shoulder into mine.

"What about it?" I smirk. "I like the view."

He eyes me up and down before his gaze follows mine all the way to Eden. "I heard you and her stayed back over break... alone."

I chuckle but say nothing. Eden has made it clear she wants to keep this under wraps for now at least, and I don't want to be the asshole that breaks her trust.

"When you're nursing a broken nose, I'll be sure to say 'I told you so'." He grins at me, and I punch his arm.

"We had to shoot some pictures and shit... it was work."

"I bet you did a lot of work, bro." he calls to me with a wink as he walks away backwards.

I shake my head in denial, but the grin across my face is probably telling an entirely different story.

Max is a good dude, I'd be dead by now if it was his sister I was messing around with, but he's more forgiving with someone else's it would appear.

I look back to Eden who offers me a smirk that's sexier than sin, and fuck it, I'll be getting close to her tonight one way or another – big brother be damned.

***

"You're not paying attention in the slightest, are you?" Brad claps his hands to try and catch my eye.

"Not particularly," I drawl as I watch Eden and her friends splashing around in the shallow water. Eden is only in up to her ankles, and I'm trying to figure out why she doesn't go deeper – I know she's brave enough now.

"Jesus Christ, Jake," he growls. "Can you at least look at me when I'm talking to you?"

I reluctantly pull my eyes from the knockout in the fire-engine-red bikini.

"What's up?"

We've gone over this shit hundreds of times. I get it. I stand on my board and surf the waves. It's not rocket science.

There's obviously more to it than that, but not to me. Surfing is like breathing. Easy. Natural.

"Alright." He drops down into the chair across from me. "Who is she?"

I smirk and consider bullshitting him, but only for half a second. Brad has been like a father to me most of my life, and I can't lie to his face. Not easily anyway.

"Her name's Eden."

He looks over my shoulder and glances at the girls. "Zeke's sister?" He whistles low. "I always knew you had balls, kid, but *damn*."

"You think I'm worried about Brady?"

He chuckles and shakes his head. "*Shit no*. But you should be worried about *her* – that girl looks like she could chew you up and spit you out and not even feel bad about it." He chuckles again and shakes his head at me like he thinks I'm mad.

"She's not so tough under that sassy exterior," I say, my eyes finding her again of their own accord.

"Careful, kid, you're starting to sound like you might be losing your head to some chick."

I don't turn, but I can hear the teasing and amusement thick in his tone.

He always warned me that this day would come.

"I'm not losing my head, Colesy." I glance at him briefly. "I've already lost it."

He claps me on the shoulder. "Best feeling in the world, isn't it?"

I chuckle and turn my back on Eden. That's not at all what I was expecting him to say.

I raise my brows at him in question. "Something you're not telling me, coach?"

As far as I'm aware, he is still as single as ever.

He chuckles and shakes his head. "Nice try, kid, but we're talking about *you*."

"We can go back to that in a min. Who's the chick? Is she hot?"

He shakes his head at me. "You're going to wish you never asked."

I open my mouth to grill him, but he cuts me off.

"Is she going to be a problem for you out there tomorrow?"

"Why would she be a problem?" I scowl at him.

I don't like Eden being referred to as 'a problem'. She's the furthest thing from it.

"You can't keep your fucking eyes off her for starters, that, and her brother is gonna kick your ass when he finds out you've been giving it to his baby sister. You don't need any trouble, you're so close."

"It's not an issue."

I hear Eden's laugh and I snap around to watch her, my own mouth tugging up into a grin as I land eyes on her smiling face.

She meets my gaze, and so much passes between us in those few seconds; secrets, lust, fuck, maybe even love.

She dips her head and I can see the blush on her cheeks.

"Oh yeah... she's going to be a *big* problem," Brad mutters. "One more day, Jake, just give me *one more day* with your head in the game and then you can get your ass kicked or live happily ever after or whatever the fuck it is that you want to do with this girl."

When I don't turn back around, he gives my leg a kick.

"Got it, coach, one more day," I mutter.

CHAPTER TWENTY-TWO

Eden

Zeke has just pulled out his trusty old guitar, and I know that this is the only chance I'm going to get. He won't notice if I slip away while he's playing.

I stand and casually stroll up the beach as he strums a Jack Johnson tune to everyone crowded around the bonfire.

I walk up the sand until I'm out of sight and sit down at the bottom of the sand dune.

It only takes a few minutes before he's right here next to me, and only seconds after that he's on top of me, pressing my back down into the sand.

I look up at him, with only the light of the moon to guide us.

"I've missed you, golden boy," I murmur as I run my hands through his hair, the way I've been dying to all day.

"I've missed you too," he whispers against my skin as he places soft kisses to my lips.

I giggle as the strands of his hair tickle my face.

"Do you know how much I've suffered, watching you prance around in that fucking bikini, knowing I can't lay a finger on you?"

"Poor baby," I coo mockingly.

I know how he feels though. Those abs of his have been tempting my tongue for hours. He *really* needs to learn how to wear a shirt.

His mouth has barely left my skin as he trails kisses along my jaw and then lowers to the swell of my breasts.

"The sooner we tell your brother about us the better. I don't want to hide you ever again."

My heart thumps in my chest, a mixture of love and fear swirling into one.

I want to tell Zeke now, I *do*, because I don't want to keep Jake a secret any more than he wants to keep me one, but I just *can't*. Not yet.

"I don't want to hide either," I whisper as I rake my hands over his bare back. I'm probably going to leave a mark, but the thought only makes me dig my nails in deeper. "But we can't tell him yet... not when you both need to focus on surfing tomorrow... I'll tell him when we get home."

He pulls back, and I can see his scowl, even in the dim moonlight.

"There is no way in hell that you're telling him without me there."

I scowl back at him. "He's *my* brother. I don't need you to hold my hand."

"And you're *my* girlfriend," he retorts, his chest heaving against mine. "And I know you don't *need* me to take care of you, precious, but I'm fucking well going to do it anyway, so you may as well get used to it."

My resolve crumbles and I tug his face to mine, pressing my lips to his. I really like the sound of being his girl.

"Fine... we'll tell him after the comp... *together*..." My heart swells. I may have had Zeke on my side all my life, but this is different – Jake is here because he wants to be, because he cares about me. He chose to be on my team.

"*Eden*," he starts again, but I cut him off with another kiss.

"I don't want to argue with you, not right now, just kiss me, please... make me yours."

He releases a pained groan and then does exactly what I've asked.

***

"Boo."

I jump into the air with fright.

I clutch my chest as she pops a brow. "Going somewhere?"

"Jesus, River, you scared the shit out of me," I snap.

"Zeke is looking for you."

"Shit." I glance around, hoping like hell that he didn't come looking this way.

"Don't worry, I covered for you – told him you'd gone up to your room to grab something warmer to put on."

I exhale in relief. Of course River covered for me.

"Wait a sec." I look back at my best friend. "How'd you know where I was?"

"I *didn't*." She sits her hands on her hips. "I *still* don't know, but it wasn't lost on me that right after you disappeared, so did Jake. Fancy *that* for a coincidence."

I wince. "Was it that obvious?"

Her eyes widen slowly, as though she didn't really believe that it was true until right in this moment. "Oh. My. God. You're really hooking up with Jake?"

I shush her and drag her by the arm up the path that will lead up to the hotel. Apparently, I need to find something warmer to wear.

"You can't say a word," I hiss at her.

She salutes me, her eyes dancing with excitement. "Hey, if you don't tell Alexi about me and Lukah, I won't tell anyone about you and the enemy boy."

I roll my eyes. "I'm serious, River, not a word."

"Scouts honour, but you better spill so hard. I need details and I need them *now*."

"I spent the whole break at his house," I whisper, and it feels so good to finally say it out loud.

I hate that I can't be open about this with the whole world right now. I hate that Jake can't take my hand on the beach like we did when it was just the two of us.

We're in a different country, at an entirely different beach, but in my mind, we're still back there in our own little bubble of sex and laughter.

I'm falling for Jake Carson the way you'd fall off the side of a sky-high building – head over heels, with no hope of return.

"Oh snap," she breathes. "You *didn't*?"

I nod. "I *did*. It sort of just happened... one thing led to another and now I don't know what to do."

"Don't let your brother find out, that's for damn sure." She giggles, but it dies off when she sees the pained look in my eyes.

"He's going to hate me," I whisper.

She squeezes my arm. "Zeke could *never* hate you... and you don't have to tell him anyway – it can be your little secret. We'll all go our separate ways in a few days and Zeke will be none the wiser."

That's the problem though. I can't imagine going back with Zeke and Millie. There's only one place I want to be, and that's with Jake.

"Holy shit." She gasps as she studies my face. "You're in love with him, aren't you?"

I shrug. "I think I might be," I reply helplessly.

"Well crap," she mutters as we reach the door of the hotel. "I don't know what to tell you, babe. I think you might be in trouble."

I'm in trouble alright, a whole damn heap of it.

***

There's a knock at my door. "Two seconds," I call out as I throw a pair of shorts over my bikini. I've only been awake for ten minutes. I had to go back down to the bonfire last night, with a jersey I didn't need on, all to keep up appearances.

I throw open the door.

I was expecting it to be Zeke, telling me he's heading down the beach to warm up for the event, and it's him alright, but there's something wrong.

"I'm only going to ask you this once, okay?" he growls.

My heart rate starts to accelerate as I take in the haunted look in his eyes.

I nod and try to keep my voice even. "Okay..."

He holds up a sheet of paper he has clutched in his hand. It's scrunched up, his fist tightly balled around it.

"What's that?" I don't know why, but my voice is barely above a whisper.

"It's the bill from the last hotel."

"Okay..." I say again.

"It says you checked out right after we left."

My heart plummets to the pit of my stomach and my palms start to sweat.

"Here comes the question, Eden, and I'd think long and hard about lying to me about this."

I try and fail to swallow the lump in my throat.

"Where did you stay all that time we were gone?"

He already knows the answer – he's figured it out, I can see it in his eyes. He wants me to confirm it for him though. He needs my answer before he acts.

"Zeke," I plead as I reach for his arm, but he shrugs me off.

"Say it, Eden."

I drop my eyes to the floor. "I stayed with Jake," I whisper.

"He's dead," he growls as he turns and barges out the door.

CHAPTER TWENTY-THREE

Jake

"Zeke, *no*!" I hear her scream, and I look up just in time to see Zeke charging through the shallow water towards where I've just come in from my warm up, Eden running down the beach after him.

He knows.

"Fuck," I mutter as his fist connects with my jaw.

My head snaps back with the impact, and in the next moment I charge at him, spearing him through the middle, sending us both flying into the shallows, closer to the shore.

We wrestle on the ground, my board still attached to my leg as Eden's screams get closer and closer.

He gets a good shot at my nose and blood sprays all over us.

I shove him and get to my feet, ripping off my leg rope as I go.

He follows me, taking another swing, but missing this time. "You're fucking dead! I'll kill you my damn self!" he thunders. "I *warned* you not to touch her, Carson."

I'm aware of a crowd forming around us. The beach is already packed, but it's too late to end this now – nothing I say could make him stop.

"Jesus Christ, Zeke, stop!" Eden is right in front of us now, she's doing her best to squeeze herself in between the two of us, but neither of us are allowing it as we shove her clear of the danger zone.

"What the fuck would you have done? Huh, Brady?" I throw my board to the sand angrily. "What would you have done if you fell in love with Millie and then her big, bad brother rolled up and told you to stay away from her?"

I shove him hard in the chest as Eden screams at us again to stop. He comes right back.

His face pales. "You're trying to tell me you're in *love* with her?" He sneers the words, as though they taste like acid rolling off his tongue.

"Of course I fucking love her!" I roar at him as I get so far in his face that our foreheads are touching. "*Look* at her. She's the most incredible woman on this whole fucking beach."

I can feel Eden clawing at me, trying to tug me back.

"Jake, *please*," she begs. "Just walk away."

I should listen to her, in fact, I'm about to let her lead me away when he drops a bomb that has my arm snapping back into a fist before I even register what I'm doing.

"You always told me you'd fuck her to get one over me, so congratulations, asshole, *you win*."

Screw this shit. This wasn't just about *fucking* her, and the fact that he's just announced that to a beach full of people has me seeing red.

As if I'd ever play with her feelings that way.

I smack him square in the face right as Brad grabs me, pulling me back so I can't go again.

Zeke lurches forward, no doubt in retaliation, but his coach is there too, holding him back in the same way.

We both struggle against them as we stare at each other, each wishing death or worse for the other.

"You said that?" a small voice, possibly the only voice that could reach me now asks.

My eyes drop to hers in a flash, my fight forgotten.

"*Eden*," I whisper. "It wasn't like that."

Her eyes well with tears. "You told my brother your goal was to fuck me one day? You said that to hurt him?"

I nod, feeling the shame fill my body.

"Did you touch me just to make him suffer?" she asks, her voice breaking. "Is that what this was to you? A game?"

"No, precious, *Jesus*... no. It's not like that," I stammer, not able to find the words to make her see that those taunts were a lifetime ago – that they had nothing to do with us – the *real* us.

"I told you he was bad news, Eden," Zeke hisses.

My eyes snap to him as his girlfriend, Millie, appears at his side.

Eden turns, her back to me now as she takes a step towards her brother. "You think I care what you *told me* right now? You've hurt me as much as he has."

"Eden," he whispers, clearly pained.

"Just go and surf, Zeke, it's what we're all here for – and clearly this little rivalry is more important to you both than my feelings could ever be, so go. *Surf*. You two want to hate each other, be my fucking guest – just leave me out of it."

She takes a step away and he tries to pull away from his coach but Millie steps in front of him. "Leave her – this is her choice."

She reaches out to cup his face, but he pulls away. "Don't touch me," he hisses. "You knew and you didn't tell me."

"Eden, please," I call to her, ignoring the newly evolving drama in front of me. She doesn't even look back as she pushes through the crowd.

"Fuck's sake, Colesy, let me go," I growl. "I'm not gonna hit him again."

Not right now anyway.

He reluctantly releases me, and I follow after her as fast as I can.

"Eden!" I yell, and she stops, slowly turning to face me.

"It wasn't like that. You have to believe me."

"It seems to me that it was *exactly* like that," she replies, her voice broken and hollow.

"Don't do this, precious, don't run, *please*," I beg her, aware that everyone can hear me desperately pleading with her.

I feel hollow.

I always knew this girl would destroy me.

"We could have had something real, you know that?" Her empty blue eyes look back at me.

I guess I've destroyed her too.

No. shit. No.

"*Could* have?" I whisper.

She stares right at me, but it's almost as though she doesn't see me.

"Yes, Jake, *could* have. Past tense. As in *before* you broke my heart."

I can't feel where Zeke hit me, but I feel the punch she just delivered directly to my chest. It's as though my heart has been blown clean out of me.

She turns around and walks away and it takes a moment of calling her name to realise that Zeke is right next to me, doing the exact same thing.

"This isn't over," Zeke growls out when she's too far away to hear. "I won't let you mess with her again."

She turns and looks at the pair of us before leaving our sight.

"I don't give a fuck what you think, Brady, but *she* does – and I care about her – so if you hurt her like that again, I'll hurt you, regardless of whether or not she's my girl."

I leave him with my warning.

***

I throw my board into the back of the tent and land heavily into a chair, my head already in my hands.

I haven't surfed that badly in my whole life.

Fucking Zeke must be feeling awfully fucking smug out there right now. It's the first time he's beaten me all tour. Even Max and Joe got the better of me.

I tug at the yellow jersey I'm wearing before throwing it off over my head.

It's a joke. I didn't surf like a champ out there just now, in fact, I surfed worse than a rookie.

She's got my head all twisted up – I didn't realise how much I needed her until she wasn't there.

It might just be some stupid ritual, but it was *ours*, and then it wasn't there, and I couldn't think straight.

It was more than some stupid kiss not being blown. It was a stark reminder that she said we were done.

Over.

Finished.

"Fuck," I grunt and punch the wall of the tent.

This is all fucked up.

I can't even keep myself sane without her.

"You about done?"

I scowl at Colesy as he drops into the seat opposite me.

"Not even remotely," I growl.

"Well you'll be done on the waves if you surf like that again."

I huff out a breath. I don't give a fuck right now.

"This really how you wanna win that title?" he asks, and I'll admit, the idea of losing here today and then being crowned the world champ feels like shit.

That's not me. I want to end the season the same way I started it – on a high.

"Zayne is watching back home, Jake. I know your head's all fucked up, but you have to get past it. For *him*. For *me*. For your fans... but most importantly for *you*, man. You've earnt this. I've never known someone who works as hard as you do – you owe it to yourself to win this thing."

"I'm a mess," I admit, dropping my head so he doesn't have to see the defeat in my eyes.

"That's women for you."

"It's just one woman, Colesy, I only want the one."

"I get that, trust me, I do. But right now, you can't think beyond the waves. You've got a few rounds before you can even consider making the finals, and you know what the real beauty of it is?"

I raise my eyes to his.

"She'll still be there when you're done winning."

"You think?" I ask in a rare moment of vulnerability.

"That girl is fucking crazy about you. I've never seen Zeke and Eden fight, but they were fighting about *you* – that's got to mean something."

I hope to god he's right.

I don't want to be a loser here. I've already made a huge scene down on the beach, the last thing I need is me surfing like shit to get people talking even more than they already are.

It's a miracle either of us were still allowed to surf today after our very public performance.

"Get your fucking board and go and show those rookies what it's like to surf with the best."

I nod my head and watch as he gets to his feet and walks away.

I think about my brother and how he looks up to me. He didn't see the punch up, thank god, but he would have seen me surf like I'd never been on a board in my life, and that's not good enough for me. I want him to see my best.

"I'm not fucking losing," I mutter under my breath.

Then I do as coach said and go show them how it's done.

CHAPTER TWENTY-FOUR

Eden

I can still picture them standing there, shoulder to shoulder, chests heaving in unison as they both called out my name – it's likely the first time they've ever been in sync about anything.

I feel so fucking stupid.

I gave him such a huge part of me, and this whole thing was just a game to him.

I close my eyes and will the tears to stay at bay as I listen to the commentator announcing the results of the heat.

I don't know why I didn't go somewhere out of earshot, but I guess I'm a sucker for punishment, because I had to know.

This is the first time since it started that I won't be there to receive Jake's kiss as he goes up against my brother, and even now that I know this whole thing was just a game, I'm still cut deep by the ritual being lost.

"What an upset, folks," the voice booms over the whole beach, "Jake Carson, current world number one has failed to score high enough in this heat to progress straight to the finals – he's going to have to slog it out through the heats – something we're yet to see this year."

The pain in my chest threatens to overwhelm me.

"Winning this round, we have Zeke Brady, coming out with a flyer early in the day and showing Jake that he's here to bring his A game."

I laugh bitterly. Zeke finally got his win over Jake. I can't help but feel like this victory is at my expense.

I listen with my eyes closed as another heat gets under way, and then another, and another.

Eventually, I hear feet to my left. I'm expecting it to be River, so when I turn and see Millie, I'm surprised.

Her eyes are red like she's been crying.

"You found me."

"I knew where you were, I just thought you might need some time." She shrugs as she sits next to me. "And I wanted to watch your brother surf, even if he's being a giant ass."

She sniffs and I nudge my knee against hers. "You okay?"

She nods and gives me a small smile.

"You knew?" I question. That's the one thing I haven't been able to figure out. Zeke yelled it at her down at the beach. He said she knew about Jake and me.

"Of course I did. One look at the two of you and I could tell." She nudges my knee back. "Plus, I'm the one who got the bill from the hotel saying you checked out... I might have pretended I hadn't seen it."

I huff out a humourless laugh and rub my hands over my face. What a mess. "It doesn't matter now anyway. They're fighting for *nothing*."

"Are they?"

I roll my head to look at her in question.

"You're miserable right now, Eden. You *love* him. I can see that from a mile away."

I don't say anything because denying it would only be a lie.

"He loves you too. The guy's so messed up he can't even surf, and that's the only thing he knows."

"I heard," I murmur as I play with a strand of grass between my fingers.

I can't see the line up from here, but I heard it all.

"But it was all just a game to him..."

"Do you really believe that? When you think about the two of you together, does it feel like he was playing with you, Eden? Because I've seen the way he watches you and I'm certain this isn't a joke to him."

It doesn't feel like a joke to me either. Under those layers of bravado, he's sweet, kind and patient. He's been nothing but good to me.

When I think about it, he was honest too – sure he never explained that he'd dangled sleeping with me under my brother's nose – but he never once lied about wanting to have me in his bed.

Maybe I overreacted. Maybe I should have given him a chance to explain.

"I'm sorry you got dragged into this," I say when I can't think of another way to answer her. "I'm sorry Zeke is mad at you."

She shakes her head. "He'll come around, Eden, he just loves you so much and the idea of losing you scares him – he doesn't know how to handle the fact that you're all grown up now."

"I'm pretty sure that throwing punches isn't it. They're lucky they didn't both get thrown out."

She nods in agreement. "Brad must have a hell of a lot of pull power with the league to have pulled that one off."

That's for damn sure.

"Go and talk to him, Eden, he can't stay mad forever."

She's right, I know she is. I need to talk to Zeke before he does something else he'll regret, something that really does tear us apart.

"What about you?" I ask as I let the grass fall to the ground. "He loves you too, he can't stay mad at you either."

She gives me another small, sad smile. "I hope not. And I think I'll stay here for a bit. It seems like a good spot to think."

I kiss her cheek and get to my feet.

"Hey, Mills?" I call to her before I leave.

She glances back at me over her shoulder.

"Thanks for having my back."

***

Because Zeke won his heat this morning, he gets a free ride into the semi finals later on today, so if I know my brother like I think I do, he'll be lazing in his room for a while, playing video games and eating pizza.

My mind lingers on the shitty food that Jake eats and I feel like crying – they have more in common than they probably realise.

I don't bother knocking – I won't get through the door if he knows it's me.

I step into the doorway of the small living area and there he is, sitting on the couch, pizza in hand – as expected.

"I hear you finally got that win over him," I say in an attempt to break the ice.

It doesn't work, he doesn't even glance at me.

"Pack your shit, I'm sending you home today," he growls.

"I'm not a child, Zeke," I say with an exhausted sigh. "You can't send me off to boarding school with a slap on the wrist."

He jumps to his feet and stalks past me. He doesn't so much as look at me once.

I sigh again and follow after him into my room.

He shoves a suitcase at me. "Pack your shit, Eden, I'm not messing around."

I take it from him and throw it on the bed.

"Fine," I accept his demand. "I'll pack. But I'm *not* leaving. You can't run my life like this, Zeke. Not anymore."

"Where are you gonna go?" He sneers at me. "To *him*?"

I start throwing my stuff into the case without answering him. There's no point, he's already made up his mind.

"You're really going to choose *him*?" he asks, and this time his voice is fully of agony.

I drop what I'm holding and look up at him, finding him looking at me for the first time since I walked in. "I shouldn't *have* to choose, Zeke, that's the god damn point. It's not a 'him or you' scenario – it doesn't have to be that way."

He shrugs at me. "It *is* that way."

I stare at him hard for a few beats before taking a deep breath and packing the rest of my stuff.

He just stands there, arms crossed stubbornly against his chest as he watches me go back and forth from the closet to my bag.

Once I'm done, I drag the big suitcase up and off the bed.

I pause as I reach his position in the doorway. "You know what? It wouldn't have killed you to ask me."

I hate the hurt and fear in my voice. Zeke and I have been through so much together, and it kills me that *this* is the thing that is going to break us apart.

He's quiet for a beat.

"Ask you *what*?" he growls.

"If I love him," I say simply.

I hear his sharp intake of breath as I pass by.

I thought I was done but decide that I'm not.

"And just for the record, the way you're treating Millie is bullshit and you know it. She did *nothing* wrong. She didn't tell you her suspicions because she knew you'd react *exactly* the way you have. She was the one who told me to come here and talk to you – she told me you'd find a way to understand, because you love me... I guess she was wrong about something after all... Good luck for your final, Z."

I reach for the door handle.

"Eden?" His voice reaches my ears, quiet and broken.

"*What*?" I reply, not turning to face him.

"*Do* you love him?" he asks, and I can hear how much it pains him to ask me this question.

I take a deep breath, and then another, and another... before turning around to face the man who practically raised me.

He already knows I do, so instead I tell him something he doesn't know.

"He got me to go back in the water, Zeke."

The words hang in the air between us, and the only way I know he heard is by the widening of his eyes.

This is a big deal. He knows that as well as I do.

It's not just about getting in the water – it's a symbol of how much I trust Jake.

"There's plenty of fish in the sea, why can't you go find another one?" he pleads, even though I can see it in his eyes that he knows he's wasting his time.

There's only one fish I'm interested in, even if things are all screwed up between us.

I drop my suitcase and take a step towards my brother.

"Except I don't go in the sea, Z. He's the only person that has got me in there in the past ten years, so there's something kind of ironic about that idea, isn't there?"

He nods his head and rakes his hand over his face.

He looks like he's about to cry. I hate it – this distance between us. He's my big brother and my best friend. I don't want to lose him.

I rush at him and throw my arms around his waist.

He releases a deep breath and then hugs me back, his chin resting on top of my head.

"I just want you to be happy, Eden, but it's hard to let go – you're all I've got left."

"Letting go doesn't mean you have to lose me. That's never going to happen."

He kisses the top of my head. "You promise?"

"I promise."

Easiest promise I ever made.

He sighs. "He said that to me, you know, about..." he winces, "*fucking* you... it was a long time ago, Eden... and he only said it because he knew I'd react."

Hope blossoms inside my chest. Millie was right.

"Thank you for telling me," I whisper.

"He really got you into the water?" he asks, pulling away and holding me at arm's length.

I nod shyly.

He shakes his head like he can't believe what he's about to say. "You better go and find him then before he loses that yellow jersey."

We both know that can't happen, but losing today would hurt Jake.

"Thank you," I breathe.

I give Zeke one last squeeze, then pull away and run, out of the hotel and down the beach, searching for him with every twist of my head.

I can't see him anywhere.

"Eden!" I hear River yell.

I scan the crowd until I see her, she's pointing out into the line up. She knows who I'm looking for.

I rake my eyes over the surfers, the boats and jet skis until I see him.

He's all alone, sitting on his board, his yellow jersey stuck tight to his wet skin.

"Jake," I whisper as I make my way to River. "I'm right here, golden boy."

CHAPTER TWENTY-FIVE

Jake

I run my hand over the cool water next to my board.

I'm up against Alexi in the semi-finals and I'm going to annihilate him. I can feel it.

There's a fire in my belly right now, something I'm not accustomed to feeling.

Where I'm normally cool, calm and collected, ever since I got back out here, I'm nothing short of a man on a mission.

In my messed-up mind, getting her back and winning are one and the same. I've decided that I won't get her back if I don't get my shit together, and so far, I have.

I've crushed everyone I've come up against. In a way, I'm glad for this detour on my way to the final.

Getting to surf more waves has never been a bad thing in my eyes, and shit, I've surfed some waves out here today.

Maybe I needed this – it's reminded me of where I've come from.

"You're up."

I turn and see coach on his jet ski, and I give him a nod of my head.

I climb on, my board tucked under my arm as he drives me into the line up.

***

A few of the guys bump their knuckles against mine as I take a seat on the boat.

It's Max's dad's – the thing is flash as hell. The dude is loaded. He's cool though, lets us hang out here in between heats.

"You want to head back to shore?" coach asks, and I know what he's really asking.

Do I want to go and find her?

I shake my head. There's no time. The final starts in ten minutes and all I have to do is beat her brother.

Again.

Then I'll come for her, and she better be ready, because if she thinks this was all just a game, that I just wanted to fuck her and move on, then she better think again.

"You sure?"

"I'm sure."

I'd give anything to see her face before I get back on that board, but I can't get on my knees and grovel before I go out there. There's no time for promises, and there definitely isn't time for another punch to the face – which is what I'd be bound to get from Zeke if I so much as looked at her.

"Alright kid." He shrugs. "Let's get this show on the road then."

I grab a tow from Colesy as my name gets cheered and yelled from every direction.

Half the guys are out here in the line up – on boats, skis, and a heap of them on boards.

I can hear the commentator telling the crowd that this is the final heat of the day and that regardless of the outcome, I'm the world champion.

I let that sink in for a minute.

I'm the best surfer in the world right now.

I could go out here and not catch a single wave and it wouldn't even fucking matter. I'd still be the best.

"You damn well did it, kid," Colesy says, and I hadn't even realised we had come to a stop.

Ever since I was little and coach used to take me out with him, I would always tell him I was going to be the best one day – that I'd be the champion of the world.

And I'm fucking here.

This moment makes up for my dad running out on me and my mum, and Zayne's dad doing the same to him – because we have *this* – we have Brad, and we have our dreams.

Who needs a fucking dad when I can show my little brother that you can do whatever the hell you like with your life?

"Quit looking all emotional. I don't know what to do with you when you're not being a cocky prick."

I chuckle and attempt to shake myself off. "I don't know either, coach."

I check my leg rope is on nice and tight as I hear the commentators announcing that the final will be getting under way in two minutes' time.

"Show time." I smirk at him.

"Hey, Jake... one last thing," he says, pointing across the line up to the jet ski that Zeke has just jumped off.

I stand up on the tow and follow his finger.

That's when I see her.

She's clinging to the life vest of Zeke's coach, Connor Smith, her sexy ass on the back of his ski.

She raises one hand and waves shyly at me.

"Nothing but fucking trouble," I hear coach mutter, but I can hear the amusement in his voice.

I shake my head and chuckle.

I'm about to raise my hand and wave back, but I think again and bring my hand to my mouth instead.

I blow her a kiss and watch as her eyes light up.

"C'mon, baby," I murmur to myself.

She slowly, ever so fucking slowly brings her hand up and just when I'm expecting her to flip me off, she surprises me by blowing me a kiss back.

She mouths the words 'I love you' to me and fuck it all, I melt. Just like that *everything* is right in my world again.

Always knew I was a simple fucking man.

I dive into the water and paddle in the direction of my opponent, my girlfriend's brother and my biggest competition out here in the waves.

I've faced a lot of guys in finals this year, but this here is the match up we deserve for the big finale.

"Hey, Brady?" I call out to him.

He turns to look at me, his usual scowl etched into his features.

I nod in the direction of his sister, who's now being sped off back to the beach.

"I'm going to *marry* your sister one day."

He flips me off and I chuckle.

Just like old times.

CHAPTER TWENTY-SIX

Eden

I run down the beach and scramble over the rocks before my feet hit the water.

Everyone else might be content to wait on the sand, but not me.

That's the man I love riding that wave towards me, and I'll be damned if I'm going to let anyone else get their hands on him before I do.

"Golden boy!" I call, and he smirks at me, that devilish smirk that has lust instantly swirling in my belly.

I wade out deeper in the water, something I never would have done if not for him.

"Hey, precious," he breathes as he stops in front of me and tucks his board under his arm.

I can't stand it a moment longer. I throw myself at him and he manages to catch me with one arm.

"I'm so fucking sorry," he growls against my ear.

"I'm the one who needs to apologise."

His green eyes search mine for any hint that I'm upset, but he'll find none.

I press up on my toes and kiss him, and the whole crowd erupts into cheers and whoops of excitement behind me.

He chuckles against my lips.

"Get a room." I hear a voice from behind Jake and I grin.

My eyes zone in on my brother's face, and I hold out my fist for him as he approaches us.

"You were so good, Z."

He bumps his knuckles against mine before looking at Jake.

"Respect, man." He holds out his hand, and I hold my breath.

They're both sporting bruises from each other's fists, so if this isn't a peace offering, I don't know what is.

Jake reaches out, and I continue holding my breath as they grip each other's hand firmly.

"Hurt her and I'll kill you, for real this time," Zeke warns him.

"Wouldn't expect anything less," Jake says.

And just like that, I breathe again as they release each other and Zeke walks towards the beach and all his fans – the new number two in the world of surfing.

Millie is right there at the front, always his biggest fan, and when he stops right in front of her and kisses her like no one else is around, I don't even get grossed out – I'm just relieved that I didn't screw up things for them.

Jake tosses his arm over my shoulder and leads me into the beach and the hundreds of people waiting to congratulate the man with the number seventeen on his back.

"Best there is, huh?" I say with a giggle. "You just had to leave it right until the bitter end."

It all came down to one last wave.

This heat was the closest they've been all year.

Jake had priority and he could have let it go – let Zeke win since the world title was already his, but that's not Jake.

He would never *let* someone win. I think deep down, Zeke respects him for that too – even though he'd never admit it.

I sure respect him for it.

He's the *best*, and the only way anyone is going to beat him is by being better than he is, that's all there is to it.

Jake kisses the top of my head before his buddies grab him and lift him clean above their heads, his board lifted alongside him in classic surf celebration.

"Hey, precious?" he calls back to me over the sea of people.

I pop a brow and wait for whatever smart ass comment he's bound to make, but it doesn't come.

"I love you too," he says with a grin, and yip, I fall just a little bit deeper.

EPILOGUE

Jake

"Ladies, please! I can't hear myself think," Millie yells at the group of us – the majority of us males, might I add – as we clink our beers together.

She's trying to talk on the phone, but I don't know why she's bothering out here – it's too god damn loud on this deck. Not helped at all by the fact that my little brother is yelling and carrying on, putting on a show.

My mum is here too – tucked up against Colesy. I eye them as I take a pull from my beer. My coach and my mother. Who the fuck saw that one coming? It's been nearly a year of seeing them together and I'm still not used to it in the slightest.

"How's it feel, bro?" Max asks me, interrupting the urge I have to rough up the man who has been my only male role model my whole life.

I suddenly feel a deep appreciation and understanding for the way Zeke reacted to me dating his sister when he found out last season.

I shake my head as I glance out at the setting sun. "I can't even explain it."

I feel like I won the lottery.

"I still reckon I could take you again though." He chuckles, and I groan.

He's never let that slide.

Here I am, winner of this leg of the tour, and world champ, for the second year running – and the bastard is still paying me out for losing to him. *Once*. A year ago.

"It's the price you pay for a good woman." I smirk, as my eyes land on said woman, strolling towards me, her friends flanking her like she's some kind of queen bee.

"I called that shit, remember?" he announces, grinning victoriously. "I always knew you were screwed when it came to that chick."

"Not even going to argue with you, bro," I reply lazily as I wait in anticipation for her to arrive. I'm as screwed now as I was then, and I'm more than okay with that.

She doesn't disappoint, dropping her sexy ass right into my lap and wrapping her long arms around my neck.

She's even sexier now than she was when I met her, and that's quite the achievement. Might have something to do with the fact that she travels with me now, and that she's back on a board – no one looks as good out there riding the waves as Eden does.

"Hey, golden boy," she practically purrs in my ear.

She's got on sweet fuck all, and *Jesus* is she tempting.

I'm just about to tell her that we need to get the hell out of here, and fast, before the bulge in my pants becomes a real problem, when Millie yells out again.

"Alright, boys, I need a favour from one of you."

We all turn to face her, and the noise dies down.

Everyone out here respects Millie. She's Eden's agent, and a lot of the other guys get paid for promotional work, so she manages most of them too – she's kind of like a camp mother to a lot of the guys – even though she's young enough to date any one of them.

"What's up, Mills?" Zeke asks her from his spot by the bar.

"I've got an old friend of mine on the phone – she works in the biz and she's looking for a surfer to pose for her calendar shoot. Anyone want to be her Mr. May?" she asks the group.

There's some chuckles and a few of the guys try to nominate their unwilling mates. There's shoves and raised hands on other people's behalfs and a few 'fuck offs', but no one is rushing to volunteer.

"Fuck yes," I call out to her. "I'll do it. Why look any further than the number one, baby?"

Eden groans. "How did I *know* you were going to put your hand up for this?" She turns her scowl from me to Millie. "You *couldn't* have asked when he wasn't around?" Eden points an accusing finger at her.

Millie shrugs, a smug smile on her face as though she knew exactly how this was going to play out.

"We're just giving the people what they want, precious."

"What if I want to do it?" Zeke calls out, challenging me, his eyes darting between me and his girlfriend. He might have come around to the idea of me and Eden, but the rivalry between us is far from lost. It's a bit like Lukah and Alexi – these boys don't ever really let go of their baby sisters.

Millie sits her hand on her hip and looks at him in a way that lets us *all* know that there is no way in hell she's going to allow that to happen.

He grins sheepishly. "All yours, Carson," he tosses back to me.

"Sold." I chuckle.

"But—" Eden tries to argue.

"No buts, baby, I'm a pro at strutting my stuff now – I learnt from the best."

I chuckle as Eden groans again.

Millie pulls the phone back up to her ear. "I got one – but you'll have to watch out, he's cocky as hell."

"Lord, help us all," Eden says dramatically.

"The cocky pro surfer." Millie giggles down the phone as she shakes her head at me and my smirk from across the space. "Yip, that will *definitely* work."

OTHER TITLES

Love like Yours Series
Rushed – Book 1
Pierced – Book 2
Hunted – Book 3
Chased – Book 4

Rock Games Novels
Paper, Scissors, Rock: Vol. 1
Hide and Seek: Vol. 2

My Heart Duet
My Heart Needs
My Heart Wants

Calendar Boys Novels
Mr. January
Mr. February
Mr. March
Mr. April
Mr. May
Mr. June

ACKNOWLEDGEMENTS

The songs that inspired this book – *Fool's Gold* – One Direction and *Aliv3* – Kings.

Thank you to everyone that has stuck with me through this series so far, I hope you liked Jake and Eden as much as the other couples. If you're new to my work, thank you for taking a chance and I hope you check out the other books – you won't be disappointed.

As always thanks to my editors – Spell Bound, my BETA readers and my street team. Also a big thanks to the bloggers who have taken the time to read and promote my books – it is really appreciated so much.

Bring on June!

ABOUT THE AUTHOR

NICOLE S. GOODIN is a romance author and mother of two from Taranaki in the North Island of New Zealand.

In mid-2015, she started to write about a group of characters who wouldn't get out of her head. Her first book, Rushed, was published in mid-2016.

Nicole enjoys long walks on the beach, pillow fights and braiding her friends' hair. She dislikes clichés, talking about herself in the third person, and people who don't understand her sense of humour.

Please feel free to contact her either via her website, email, Instagram, Twitter or on her Facebook page, she would love to hear your feedback. If you're feeling really game, you can even sign up for her newsletter.

Visit www.nicolegoodinauthor.com for more information.

UPCOMING TITLES

Calendar Boys Novels

Mr. June
Mr. July
Mr. August
Mr. September
Mr. October
Mr. November
Mr. December